Spirit Lake Payback

Stuart L. Scott

Moscow, Idaho

Spirit Lake Payback

Stuart L. Scott
Moscow, Idaho

Published by
Stuart L. Scott
112 S. Main St.
Moscow, Idaho

Copyright Stuart L. Scott, 2020

Printed by Amazon

ISBN# 978-1-7322468-7-4

Cover Design by: Tania Suarez Mendoza

This is a work of fiction. Many the characters were inspired by people I met professionally but the events are fictionalized and do not represent actions attributable to any specific person living or dead.

Contents

This Book is Dedicated to:

Harold and Eleanor Green, brother and sister, Auschwitz survivors who lived across the street from my parents.

My father-in-law, Stanley Vernon Wilson Junior, Private First Class in the 101st Airborne, who participated in liberating the Bergen-Belsen concentration camp as a recorder and translator of what we found there.

My uncle, William James Black, who along with my Dad, showed me what makes a man. His B-24 was shot down over Peenemünde, Germany. He was rescued by the Danish underground and later became a fighter pilot during the Korean War, retiring as a Lieutenant Colonel.

Prologue: Spokane, Washington

June 6, 1995

The Spokane newspaper article ran under the banner, Residents Rush to Plug Leaky Lake.

"It was only last week that this reporter's boat was in the water, but now it's beached on weeds and mud, here next to my dock. State officials aren't sure why the lake is leaking, but they know it's leaking a lot of water into the Spokane aquifer. The state believes that holes are the main problem. The spokesman for the Idaho Department of Lands explained. 'It's tough to tell legitimate holes from the occasional moose footprint, or one dug by a toad when the lakebed was dry. The trick is to stir up some muck near a suspected hole. If it gets sucked down, the hole is declared a "leaker" and resealed. Unless you see it happen, it's hard to believe.'"

June 10, 1995

Today the follow-up newspaper headline was an eye catcher. Spirit Lake Sink Hole Collapses to Reveal Skeletal Remains.

"Idaho authorities interrupted the efforts of local homeowners to seal the continuing plague of sink holes when an undetermined number of human skeletons were discovered in the bottom muck of a collapsed sink hole. A 250 ft. area on the south shore of the lake has been cordoned off. State and tribal archeologists are preparing to excavate the site, hoping to determine the provenance of the apparent ancient burial ground."

June 30, 1995

Spirit Lake Sink Hole Linked to Mob Body Dump.

The Kootenai County Sheriff in his lakeside press conference revealed, "Those remains appear to be 40 to 60 years old and not a tribal burial ground as we first imagined. The archeological excavation has yielded up scraps of clothing and shoes that confirm the approximate age of the remains. The Coeur d'Alene tribal Archeologist called us in yesterday when he removed a skull from the pit and noticed fillings and gold teeth. Once the site is excavated, the identification of the remains will begin. Until that time, we have a bit of a mystery on our hands."

A combined local, state and federal multi-agency task force recovered nine bodies from their Spirit Lake dump site. Skeletal remains had become disarticulated into a pile of anonymous bones, awaiting re-assembly. When they were dumped was a mystery, but bullet holes in many of the skulls and cut marks on bones all pointed to violent ends for the nine unknowns.

1. Dorris, California, March 1944

When the stranger stepped off the bus he was hit by the prevailing 20 mile-per-hour wind. A blast of fine grit left a patina on his skin and clothes. Dorris had a single paved street, a post office, a store, and a bar with what passed for food options. He took a room at the motel. The proprietress was happy to have it rented.

After dinner, not yet ready to surrender to the solitude of a cheap room alone, he walked out along the road toward the next town. It was a warm night; crickets chirped, and the smell of sage filled the air.

"Livestock" read the sign with an arrow pointing along the road. A mile out, a small house, all alight, came into view. He walked toward it.

Mildred perched in a glider swing on the covered front porch, watching the man approach. She turned and smiled as he walked past. The stranger didn't look like most of her customers. He wasn't a GI from the internment camp, a fat trucker or an old rancher. This one looked like he could pay and might even be fun.

"Are you looking for company, darling? I'm a virgin. I'm clean." She put a cigarette to her lips, trying to look both helpless and seductive. "Can you light me up? I'm out of matches," she purred keeping her eyes on the stranger. She hoped he was horny because sure as shit she didn't want to go back inside.

Walking over to the glider swing, he lit her cigarette. The girl patted the seat without speaking. She tossed her peroxide blonde hair back with a gesture she learned from a movie, hoping this John liked what he saw. A robe, too large by half, covered her from neck to mid-ankle.

"I'm Mary."

Tapping off the cigarette ash on the arm of the swing, she moved her knee just enough that her pink chenille robe drifted open to display a pale thigh. Small wisps of red hair curled out from under the hem. That was all he got for free.

"Five dollars, what do you think? You'll be glad you did."

The man smiled, fixing her with his eyes. No words passed between them as his thumb tamped tobacco into a briar pipe.

I hope his stem is longer than his pipe's. "I really am a virgin. I had a riding accident once, ." She tilted her head. "You believe me, don't you, Mister?"

"Thanks for the offer. I'm just walking before I head in for the night. You know, Mary, you can do better than this. Maybe go to Portland or Tacoma and get a job in a defense plant. They need virgins to help with the war effort." He smiled and lit his pipe as he stepped off the porch.

She liked his company and the smell of his pipe. If he walked away now she'd be left alone with her regrets and the prospect of going back inside, only to be ordered around.

"Don't go. I'm lonely. If I go back inside, the old bag that runs the place will boss me around and make me clean the kitchen. How about $3? I'm worth it; you'll see."

He kicked rocks with the toe of his boot and turned toward town. "I'm Pat McBride, Mary. I just want to walk, but thanks. You're a lovely young woman."

"Listen, take me back to town with you, and I'll do yah for free. You're right. I hate this place, and I want to be somewhere else—be somebody else." Her voice dropped as she switched from trying to sell herself to trying to save herself.

"I'm actually Mildred, from Madras, Oregon. Pretty darn dull, don't you think? Madras is the only place I know that's worse than here. The whole dump smells like you need to check the bottom of your shoes. There's nothing out there but jack rabbits and cows. If I'd stayed around Madras, I might have ended up the pump for some old rancher. If I was lucky, he'd only smack me around when he got too drunk to get it up. So, I took off as soon as I was old enough to butcher, if you know what I mean."

He walked back to the swing, reached out and put his hand on her shoulder. "You're fine, Mildred. You'll make it out of this prison. I can see that you're better than this place or this job." Then he bent, kissed her hand, and walked off.

He was not what Mildred had expected. *Maybe white knights really do exist.*

* * * *

5

The next afternoon, Clem, the local taxi driver, parked his truck in front of the little house. Mildred, watching through the window, felt something stir inside. *Why is he here? What's going to happen?*

Pat McBride got out, walked onto the porch, and opened the screen door. He knocked on the wooden frame and Della the Madam, in her usual flowered dress, went to answer.

"Welcome stranger; come on in and have a look at the new livestock." She gestured to a parlor inside to the right.

McBride hesitated and moved back a step, his eyes squinting.

Mildred bit back a giggle. Della's perfume was definitely not subtle and inviting; it reminded her of a fruit salad left too long in the sun.

"I borrowed a lighter from one of your girls, last night: Mary. I want to return it if she's not busy at the moment."

"I'll give it to her, darling," offered the madam.

"I'd like to thank her myself." Courtesy was not moving the madam, so he added, "And to arrange something with her for later tonight."

He took another step back as Della smiled and turned. She motioned for Mildred to go outside. Her look was half encouragement, half threat.

"Well, look who came back. Saw something you liked last night?" She was wearing the same pink robe. It was almost all she had.

"Listen for a minute," he said in a soft voice. "I don't want the madam to hear."

He put his hand into the pocket of her robe and withdrew it quickly. "That's all the cash I can spare."

Mildred's hand went into the pocket. Her fingers encountered a tightly folded wad of bills.

"You're fine, just who you are," he said.

"Take me with you, Mister, please."

"Darling girl, I can't take you. I'm headed to Vallejo, California to work at a shipyard."

Then he kissed her cheek before turning back to the truck.

She hit the screen door so hard in her rush that the frame smacked Della's prized beaded lamp. No time to waste. She ran to her room and grabbed all her worldly goods. On went her only pair of jeans. She didn't own a suitcase, so a pillowcase would have to do. In went her one small drawer of clean clothes and the straight razor she'd stolen from Dad. *If I don't hurry he'll be gone, and I'll have to deal with the madam!* Out the door at a dead run she went.

The truck was starting to pull away. Mildred was alone between worlds now, barefoot, in blue jeans and a robe. She clutched the pillowcase filled with everything she owned, trying to stuff her one faded blouse in as she ran.

Up ahead in the truck, Pat was staring straight ahead. Panic seized her chest. This stranger was the first man in a long time who'd been nice to her. *First, he gave me options for a better future, then money, and for what? It wasn't for my body, so for what, then? If this isn't my chance, I'm not about to wait around for another one.* She began running after the truck.

Clem, let up on the gas and leaned out the window. "God damn it," he bellowed, waving at her. "Go back, you silly bitch!"

Now she was gaining. Her robe flapping, she sprinted through the cloud of dust behind the truck until she tripped and fell into the dirt.

"Damn it!" she yelled. Her jeans and robe were now filthy. It didn't matter. On her feet once more, she watched the truck continue down the road. One quick glance back to the house and she knew which way to go. She grabbed up her pillowcase and again started running after the truck. Ten steps later one of her bare feet landed on a sharp rock and down she went, face first onto the dirt road.

"Ow-ow-ow!" Her cry came out automatically. Pain filled her body as she rolled over, hugging her knees to her chin. Wiping her face, her hand came away muddy with road dust and tears.

She coughed from her own dust cloud and spit out a brown glob of dust and saliva. Her knee was bleeding and so were the tops of several toes. Funny, but the blood didn't matter now. She got up: first to her knees, then she managed to stagger to her feet and limp on.

The truck pulled to the shoulder of the road. Then it stopped.

All she could do now was limp forward. Her jeans were torn, and blood began to fill deep scratches on her right knee. All that mattered was straight ahead. *I'll limp or crawl if I have to, but I am never turning back.*

Then the truck door opened, and Pat was jogging back towards her.

Pat grabbed her by the shoulders. They stood there in the middle of the road, wordless. He held Mildred at arm's length and regarded her.

He looked down, and his face twisted when he saw the blood.

She didn't care that her robe hung open, its seams falling straight down across what little cleavage she had. Her chest rose and fell as she sobbed and tried to catch her breath as they stood together in the middle of road.

"I can't go back. I'll kill myself rather than be a whore anymore."

Pat must have believed her, because he picked up the sack from the dirt road, pulled out the faded blouse and passed it to her.

"Get dressed." He turned his back.

Why turn away? He must have seen naked women before, and God only knows how many strange men have watched me get naked right in front of them. Doesn't he want to see my body?

She pulled on the blouse. "Ok, you can look."

Then the man who'd been a perfect stranger less than 24 hours ago put his arm around her shoulders and together they walked to the cab of the truck. She sat between Pat and the driver. Pat nodded to Clem.

"Back to the motel."

They pulled up at the motel in Dorris. She knew it because she'd tricked out of there for a few days when she first hit town.

"Go have coffee. We'll leave in half an hour," Pat told his driver. Then he turned to Mildred and pointed to a second-floor door.

"Go up to my room and clean yourself up as best you can. I'll be along in a minute." He passed her the room key. She headed up the stairs, her mind in a whirl. *He must have believed me when I said I'd kill myself. But why help me at all?*

When he came back to the room, he was carrying a couple of bags and a small man's windbreaker. She was at the bathroom sink. She'd cleaned her face with a damp cloth and was starting on her bloody knee. Wet, blonde hair hung like a white shower cap over her head.

"Sit here," he said, pointing to the toilet, and she sat on the lid.

Taking peroxide and gauze from one paper bag, he cleaned her knee and toes. Through the sting of the cleaning, Mildred made not a sound and never took her eyes off Pat. He knelt at her feet and gently encased her wounded toes in protective gauze.

"Why are you doing this?" was all she asked.

He shook his head. "See if you can wear these." He took white socks and canvas shoes from the other bag. "I'm going to write a letter. Then it's time for us to go. We have buses to catch."

From the single drawer of the small desk he retrieved a pencil, a sheet of paper and an envelope. He wrote briefly, then put the letter into the envelope. Just before handing it over to her, he wrote something on the outside.

He put the room key down on the desk and passed over the denim windbreaker. It smelled new and fresh. She put it on, wondering at the feel of the crisp cloth.

When they walked outside, Clem was waiting. Pat put his suitcase in the truck bed. Then he extended his hand and took her pillowcase poke, placing it in the pickup box next to his suitcase.

The three rode in silence to Klamath Falls. Outside the Greyhound depot, Pat handed Clem a folded $20 bill, and they got out.

As Clem drove off, they walked into the store that displayed the Greyhound Bus logo in its window. He bought a one-way ticket to Seattle for Mildred and asked its departure times. There were thirty minutes until her bus pulled in and another hour wait after that for his own bus to arrive. They went back outside and sat down on the worn wooden bench.

"Here's the deal," he said, handing over the ticket. She held it beside the letter, studying each before starting to speak.

"Don't." He squeezed her hand. "This is all I can do for you: give you a new start. You're not a whore anymore.

You get to be a virgin again. Your past stays here. Remember the riding accident." They waited, holding hands in silence, until the Seattle bus arrived.

"Find a nice guy who'll treat you like a lady. Don't settle for anything less. Now, get on the bus."

Mildred climbed the two steps, showed her ticket to the driver and walked down the aisle to a seat. For a moment they looked at each other through the bus window. Then he was gone.

2. Keyport, Washington March 1944

From the window, Mildred had watched her savior standing outside the depot. He didn't wave as the bus pulled out. Her shock at today's turn of events had not yet changed from wonderment to sheer terror of what lay ahead for her in Keyport. *It has to be better than being a piece of meat, hung out for display and sold.*

"Good afternoon." The man in the Greyhound cap crouched down to her eye level. "I'm Louie; nice to meet you. My partner, Roy, is taking his turn at the wheel. Tomorrow there'll be a one-hour breakfast stop in The Dalles at 8:00 A.M. We expect to have you in Seattle at two o'clock. This bus has a restroom in the back and your seat reclines." He pointed to a handle next to the aisle, below the seat cushion. "It might help if you're trying to sleep while we roll through Oregon."

Mildred folded the bus ticket and put it in the front pocket of her torn blue jeans. She'd tucked her pillowcase luggage into an open overhead tray that ran the length of the bus. That left one lone item in her hand, the sealed letter she'd received from her benefactor. The envelope, bent by her tight grip, bore the impression of each finger. Alone, amid quiet strangers, Mildred unfolded the paper from her fist. For the first time she read the message written on the envelope.

'At the Seattle terminal, go downstairs and take the Black Ball Ferry to Keyport. See Mrs. Lena Olson at the mercantile. Give Mrs. Olson this letter. If the store is closed, go to the café and ask for Florence.'

Should I open the envelope and read the letter? No, Mildred had decided to trust Pat McBride when she ran after him barefoot and half dressed. She'd committed to changing her life. Pat had answered her plea by offering redemptive change to a young blonde stranger he only knew as Mildred from Madras.

When he put money in her pocket, not in trade for sex, she'd marked him as a savior. Counting the money for the first time, Mildred found $17. She'd be able to eat tomorrow morning and buy the ferry ticket. As she watched the high, Eastern Oregon desert roll by, Pat's words came back to her.

"You're fine. Today I planned to save a girl from prison. I didn't know that the girl would be you or that this was the prison. We do what we think we have to do. Sometimes we do it wrong, I know. I hope you get it right next time."

Now she had received money, compassion, and hope, all freely given by a stranger. Mildred had told potential customers that she was Mary, a virgin. Somehow, riding across the high desert, she felt more like Mary Magdalene, another young whore who was touched by a stranger.

* * * *

Twenty–six hours later, the Greyhound pulled into the Metro-Seattle Transit Station. Fed and rested by her dreamless sleep, Mildred got off the bus, pillowcase in hand. She followed the signs through the station, descending the wide stairs down again to the ferry level at the harbor's edge. The smell of diesel smoke, the sounds of the city, the horns and clangs of the ferry boats filled her senses. As she walked, one hand still clutched the precious envelope. Her future hinged on the contents of the unread letter she carried in her pocket.

As Pat's instructions directed, Mildred purchased a ticket at the Black Ball Ferry kiosk. Her boarding time was in 30 minutes, so she wandered outside to the wharf. The newness of Seattle was wondrous compared to the world she'd known, between Madras, Oregon and Dorris, California.

As she rode the ferry into Liberty Bay, new sights and sounds filled her with wonder. There was so much world out here beyond the dust and scab lands between Madras and Dorris. The newness of everything left no room for fear of the unknown lying just ahead.

The ferry dock at Keyport—narrow, long and empty— rushed toward her as the ferry reversed its engines to slow its forward progress. Pillowcase in hand, Mildred made her way from the open upper deck to the boat deck and outside into the bright light of day. The clean breeze from the crossing gave way to the smells of kelp and dirty foam that lapped at the pier's pilings. As she stepped off the ferry and onto the Keyport dock, four other travelers passed her, on their unknown paths to work or home. Mildred stopped to survey the town.

She was fed, safely out of bodily servitude and had navigated a 600-mile journey. Before her she recognized a new mystery. Quiet, clean and with strangers who smiled at her, Keyport might be what she was seeking when she ran barefoot down a dusty road outside of Dorris, California.

A worn black ribbon of asphalt that began where the dock ended forked to the left and led her eyes to the entrance of the *'Naval Torpedo Station – Keyport.'* The name was spelled out in large brass letters, affixed to a low stone wall. Two sandbagged machinegun nests flanked the heavy iron gates that blocked the road into the station. Marine guards were visible in and around a small guard shack outside the gates. Opposite the guards was a three-sided bus shelter. Four souls sat on the single bench under its cover.

Mildred's gaze began to move, surveying the town. The strangers from the bus shelter passed her as they went to board the ferry. A woman and two young boys came onto the dock. The woman smiled and said a brief "Hello" as she struggled to hold on to her sons' hands. The noises of the ferry beckoned the boys to the outer limits of their mother's control.

Mildred searched for another clue about where to go. Only two buildings, one to the right and one to the left, overlooked the dock and the bay. On the left, the painted wooden sign announced, 'Smith's Café.' A second smaller metal sign was fixed to the wall by the glass entry door: 'U.S. Post Office.'

To the right of the dock sat a large building. A single gas pump stood between a covered wooden porch and a gravel strip angling off from the asphalt. Above the porch the sign read 'Keyport Mercantile.' This was it. Lena Olson would either help her or take one look and turn her away. The last few steps to the Mercantile required no t, only courage.

From the worn wooden porch, Mildred shaded her eyes and stared into the store. Amid the products that lined the walls a figure was placing cans of food on the grocery shelves. With the box now empty of its contents, the woman stood and stretched her back in a graceful backward arch.

* * * *

Lena Olson tilted her head back and noticed a girl framed by the window. Lena smiled and continued her task. There was no shortage of work for the combination owner, clerk, stocker, and janitress.

When the shopkeeper next looked up, the stranger had not moved. After another stretch, Lena left her task and walked to the entry. She pushed open the screen door, and the girl extended her arm to show a letter. Lena took it. After a long moment she opened it and read her former tenant's few words. She knew that Pat McBride had helped the War Department during his time in Keyport. Looking up from the page, she broke their mutual silence.

"It gets cool when that afternoon breeze comes across the bay; let's go inside. Do you have a suitcase?" Mildred shook her head and held out the pillowcase containing all her worldly goods.

"No worry; what's your last name?"

"Mercer."

The Olsons had no children. That mattered not to the hard-wired maternal instincts Lena carried. She shut the interior door and turned over the 'OPEN' sign to 'CLOSED'.

"I think hot tea would be good. What do you think?"

Mildred replied with a simple "Yes" and followed Lena up a flight of stairs to the Olson residence above the Mercantile.

They emerged from the hallway into the kitchen, a large room, well lit by windows on two sides. Cabinets, counter, cupboards, a double sink, and a beige Wedgewood stove lined the walls. An oversized round wooden table filled the center of the room. Lena gestured for Mildred to take a seat as she filled a tea kettle at one of the porcelain sinks. Pot filled, she placed it on a back burner of the Wedgewood. With a wooden match from a tin matchbox holder, Lena lit a front burner and slid the copper kettle over the glowing circle of blue-tipped flames.

The childless mother and the motherless child occupied the same space, but both were at a loss for words. Lena pulled cups, saucers, and spoons from their places. A box of Lipton tea bags and a tin of homemade cookies appeared. She took a seat one chair away from her unexpected company.

Mildred was the first to speak. "Bathroom, please," and she scooted her chair back to stand. She stood head down as she spoke, "I need a pad, if you have one, please." She was embarrassed by her own request, but also she thought it made her appear needier and more vulnerable.

Lena gave a sympathetic smile. *What girl does know her cycle to the very day?*

"At the house, we shared a community bathroom and there was always a box under the sink. When I went to the bus station, I only remembered then and there was no time to go back for things. I forgot my toothbrush too and had to rely on Juicy Fruit gum for my breath on the bus ride up."

Lena rose from her chair. Placing her arm around the teen's shoulders, she led down a short hall to the bathroom. Inside, she opened a tiled cabinet and pointed to an open-topped box. "There. I'll be in the kitchen making our tea." Patting the girl's narrow shoulders, Lena closed the door as she left.

When Mildred returned, the kitchen was warm from the heat of the stove. Lena met her with a smile. "Tea's ready and the cookies are fresh." Mildred sat down as Lena poured, then joined her at the table.

"After tea, you can freshen up and I'll fix up a bed for tonight." They sipped their tea before more was said. Lena read the teen's body language and could tell that gentle inquiry was best for now. Harder questions would be held for another day. She gently questioned, accepting whatever few words Mildred offered in reply to her queries.

Unspoken was Lena's need to share Pat McBride's letter with her husband. Maternal feelings aside, this was not her decision alone. Sensing the emotional limits of the girl had been reached, Lena moved on to getting her settled for the night. She ushered Mildred into the guest room, across the hall from the family bath.

"This is your room while we figure out a future plan."

* * * *

In the guest room Mildred saw simple things she'd never known. Wallpaper with tiny pink roses, a quilted bedspread folded to hold two pillows next to the ornate, white iron headboard. A round, braided rug covered the hardwood floor and filled all but the corners of the room. Across from the foot of the bed, a dark wood chest of drawers and a women's dressing table filled the wall.

When Lena looked again, Mildred was staring at her reflection in the dressing-table mirror. Unconcealed tears ran down her cheeks.

"My husband, Charles, is at work until eight tonight. This is a good time for you to have a bath. I bet that would feel good after your long trip. There's shampoo by the tub and towels in the cabinet above where I showed you." Before she could step to the door, the girl grabbed her in a tight hug and buried her face in the older woman's shoulder. Denied a child of her own, Lena enfolded the waif in her arms as she cried. The embrace lasted as long as their mutual needs required. With a squeeze of the teen's narrow shoulders, Lena stepped back.

"Do you have any clean clothes in your sack?"

Mildred dropped her gaze before speaking, "No, only underpants and a robe."

Moving one hand from her shoulder, Lena lifted the tear-stained chin. There was no "You poor thing," or other well-intentioned words of pity. "How about I find you some things from the store? You happen to have come into the finest selection of women's wear in all Keyport!" The joke brought a smile to both their faces.

"I'm guessing that you are a size 4 dress, and maybe 32-A for a brassiere? Does that sound right?" Given no answer, she tapped the underside of Mildred's chin with her index finger. "What?"

"I don't know my store sizes in things. I never had clothes from a store. My mom made my things while she was around. When she passed, I wore what didn't fit my sister or what a neighbor lady gave me."

"That's OK; I sew, so we'll use my best guesses for sizes. If I guess wrong, I'll take them back for a full refund." They both laughed. "Does the bra size sound right?" The question took the smile from Mildred's lips, so Lena tapped her again. "What?"

"I've never had one of those."

"Well, darling, it's time you did. You don't want to be tucking them in your belt when you're my age." Lena turned, giving Mildred a final pat. "Leave it to me. You bathe while I shop. I'll put your fresh things on your bed. Then I'll be in the kitchen when you're ready."

After her bath, Mildred found new clothes laid out on the bed. Three sets of underwear, short socks, and a brassiere lay next to a yellow cotton dress. On top lay a toothbrush, comb, and hairbrush. She caressed the fabrics with her fingertip, amazed by the smoothness of simple new clothes.

After hanging up her dusty pink chenille robe, Mildred started to dress but stopped to study herself in the dressing-table mirror. She marveled at the wonder of a white cotton brassiere. It would take some getting used to. She tugged at the straps and contorted her shoulders, trying to make the strangeness of this adult bodily confinement thing go away.

The enervating joy of soaking in hot water had softened the scabs on her knee and foot. She passed on wearing the new cotton socks lest blood stains soil them, using the last of the gauze to wrap her toes before gingerly putting on the canvas shoes Pat had provided.

Dressed now, Mildred combed her shoulder-length bleached-blonde hair, noticing its red roots were visible. Her traveling clothes—jeans, blouse, shoes, and underpants—all needed washing. She loaded them back into her pillowcase bag. The torn jeans, robe, and holey underwear were equal candidates for washing or burning. Next, the small bottle of peroxide went onto the dressing table.

From the bottom of the sack she withdrew a straight razor, stolen from her father back in Madras when she ran away from home. The H. Boker brand name was engraved along the top edge of the bright, four-inch steel blade. After fingering the razor's edge, Mildred placed it under her new underwear in the dresser drawer.

Only once had she needed to bring out the blade. The fear and loathing of that moment came roaring back. She remembered lying naked on her whorehouse bed and the powerless feeling of being grabbed by rough hands.

"Now I'm going to get me some of that round brown," and he lifted her hips, rolling her over, forcing Mildred to kneel butt up. From under her pillow, out came the razor. With the strength that adrenaline provides, Mildred had rolled, turned and laid the blade along his erect penis.

"You want some of that? But you'll get some of this!" She was going to turn the stud into a gelding. Her yells and his screams brought Madam Della with the axe handle she kept by the front door. Della's morality was situational, but she knew business. Customers came and went, but good young livestock was hard to find. Since the cutting had not yet begun, the John escaped intact.

The razor had gone back under her whorehouse pillow. There it slept, unneeded but never forgotten. Mildred would occasionally lift the pillow that covered its four inches of bright steel. In her darkest moments she knew Mr. Boker was a final way out. One kiss to her own white neck and nothing would hurt anymore.

* * * *

"Well look at you." Lena Olson stopped her dinner preparation to turn and admire the transformation clothes and a bath had made. "How did I do on the sizes?" Mildred beamed a smile in response. Taking the hem of the yellow dress between fingers and thumbs, she made a slow turn to show off her new outfit.

"I need to pay for the nice things. I have money left."

"Those few things are a 'welcome to Keyport' gift. You know, I get it all wholesale," Lena kidded.

"Thank you so much, everything fits fine." She pinched through the dress with two fingers to tug at the unfamiliar confining harness bedeviling her chest.

"You'll get used to it, I promise. Would you like to help set the table? Charles will be home soon."

"Yes ma'am. Tomorrow can I wash my old clothes?"

"Sure, you can, and I want to introduce you to our neighbors. You need to meet Florence at the diner and Dan, our postman. After that we'll do more shopping and planning. Does that sound all right to you?"

Mildred nodded in agreement, appreciating how she was being asked and not just told.

"Now, I'll tend the stove. The silver is here, napkins there, plates and glasses over on that wall." Lena walked as she spoke and pointed to each storage space.

"I hear my husband coming up the outside steps. You'll be a bit of a surprise. It's best if I share Pat's letter with him first thing."

"How about I go finish unpacking? And I'll repack if he doesn't like guests. You've already been so kind. I don't want to make trouble for you. I'll be in my room." Mildred put down the handful of silverware she'd been setting out, hugged Lena and left the kitchen.

* * * *

"Something smells real good!" The savory aroma of pot roast welcomed him from the doorway at the top of the stairs from the side yard.

Lena crossed their living room and planted a kiss on her husband's cheek. Charles Olson was still trim at age 47 and his straight-backed posture emphasized his full six feet. Twenty-seven years of marriage to his high school sweetheart had not dimmed his love and appreciation for Lena's beauty and her dedication to their home.

"Come sit with me. We need to talk," she said, helping her husband out of his beige windbreaker. "Everything is fine. I'll get us both a drink and tell you all about it."

"Oh yes, coffee, please." Charles trusted his wife, whatever was going on.

"I think you'll want something stronger."

"Okay," was his only response as they walked hand in hand to the kitchen. Lena gestured for him to take his customary place at the table. She poured them both a cold shot of Aquavit, the water-clear Norwegian vodka flavored with caraway. She started to put the bottle back into the refrigerator. Changing her mind, Lena poured more into both their glasses. She handed Charles his drink and took her seat next to him. Still in love, they preferred to sit side by side at meals. Lena removed Pat McBride's letter from the pocket of her gingham apron and passed it to Charles.

He read the letter in silence.

> Dear Mrs. Olson,
> I need a big favor. This is my friend Mildred from Madras, Oregon. She needs a job and a safe place to stay. I'd appreciate anything that you or Florence could do for her. She's a good person who just needs a little help.
> Thanks for everything,
> Pat McBride

After a few moments Charles put the letter down. He took a sip of Aquavit and rotated the glass in his fingers, smudging its frosty jacket of condensation.

"You and I both thought a lot of Pat. He was a good tenant for you, and he helped me at work, more times than I've told you. He's a real good fella." Charles paused for another sip from the cold, clear liquid. "So, tell me about her."

"She showed up at the store late this afternoon. She stared from the porch until I beckoned her inside. Her jeans were torn, and I saw a fresh scab on her knee. The picture was right out of one of our books from church, a motherless waif seeking shelter from her life of storms. She looked like such a lost sheep I couldn't help but invite her in. I guess it was the 'Inner Mom' in me.

"I got her a few essentials from the store and after a bath she's starting to open up. She was helping me by setting the table when we heard you coming up the stairs. I asked her," and Lena checked herself. "No, actually she offered to wait in the guest room while you and I talked. She said she'd pack up and go if you had any problem with her being here."

"Hon, I'm fine with whatever you decide." He clicked the rim of his frosty glass against his wife's drink. "We need to see where this goes. But if Pat sent her here that's enough for me, for now at least."

Lena leaned over and kissed her husband's cheek.

He rose. "Well, I'll go invite our guest to dinner."

Charles knocked on the bedroom door and asked if he could come in. The voice from inside replied, "Yes," and he opened the door. Mildred was sitting on the still-made bed. The pillowcase bag sat on the floor beside her feet. Afraid that his entry into the room might frighten this sparrow of a girl, he stayed in the doorway and gave her his most welcoming smile.

"Dinner's ready, please come join us. I'm Charles." He stepped back as Mildred got up. Stepping into the hallway, she offered her hand out to shake. But instead, he patted her on the shoulder. "Welcome."

* * * *

Mildred followed Mr. Olson back to the warm kitchen. She was surprised by what she saw. In Madras, she'd been the one to do the setting and fetching as far back as she could recall. Then at Madam Della's, it had been every girl for herself.

Lena had set three plates on the table with water glasses at their two places and an empty glass at the third. "Tonight, you get the special treatment. Yours is the red guest plate. Sit. What would you like to drink? There's ice water, milk or coffee."

Another softening in her armor; she chose milk.

When they were all seated at the round wood table, Charles to Lena's right and the guest to her left, Lena spoke again. "We say Grace before we eat. Please join us," and Mildred joined in this new ritual of prayer.

Dinner-table conversation was an unknown commodity at Mildred's house or the whorehouse. In Madras, after Mom passed, meals were silent except for the demands her father issued. "Get me another beer— more stew—clean up this place."

The Olsons asked about each other's day before turning to Mildred. Their questions were routine enough. Where was she from, about her family, and how she'd met Pat McBride. Mildred worried, not knowing what Pat may have communicated to Keyport unbeknownst to her. With her mind racing, she also worried about what might come out later that made a lie out of things she said now. But not answering now was worse than her best calculated half-truth.

"Pat came into where I was working in Dorris, California. He was out for a walk and I wasn't busy, so we had a nice conversation. I told him I wanted to get away from the dust of that small town. He came back two days later. We talked more, and he offered to help me to a bigger place with more opportunity. He suggested Keyport and said if I was serious he'd pay my way and introduce me to people he knew."

"That sounds like Pat, doesn't it, Lena? He helped me with issues at the station several times."

"And he took such good care of Duano, the man he shared our rental with," chimed in Lena. Pointing out into the darkness beyond the kitchen window she added, "Over there." Then came the question Mildred feared the most. "So, where were you working?"

"The sign out front said 'Livestock.' But it was a meat market. I sold pieces of meat. I got room and board but not much else." The string of half-truths seemed a good compromise between honesty and necessary concealment.

The Olsons smiled at one another, accepting her response. Mildred felt her underarms grow damp as she waited for the follow-up questions she feared. But none came. She was vouched safe by Pat McBride, so her brief answers sufficed.

When the meal was over, Lena said, "You wash and I'll dry," to Charles as she stood up at her place. He smiled, nodded and began to rise. Mildred didn't wait.

"What can I do to help? Clear the table? Wash or dry?"

Both the adults smiled at her unprompted offer. It was the right thing to do. Lena was glad to see the girl wanting to be a good guest or even perhaps a family member.

"Mr. Olson, why don't you go put your feet up. I'll help Mrs. Olson."

Charles smiled and complied.

First Mildred cleared the table and when done with that task, unbidden, she picked up a dish towel and began to dry the dishes that Lena passed over. Working side by side they shared comfortable small talk about their dinner. When the chores were done, Lena smiled her thanks and said, "I'll see you at breakfast. Sleep well."

Lena hoped her fears about Charles's response to their surprise guest were unfounded. She'd soon find out now that she and Charles were alone, back at the kitchen table.

"Well, what do you think?"

"She's certainly polite enough."

"I'm glad you're not mad at me for inviting the young stranger into our house and all."

"No, she's fine. You did the right thing. How about you keep a close eye on her and if her attitude stays good, she's welcome to stay."

"Thank you for trusting me, Hon. I'm not going to give her a list of rules because I don't think she needs that. I'll just sort of quietly test her. She's still pretty fragile." As they headed off to their bed, Charles added, "I can see why Pat helped her. He's that kind of guy."

3. A New Name for a New Life

The next morning Mildred made sure she got to the kitchen and had the breakfast table ready when Lena arrived. With the table set, other aspects of the meal were not her choices to make so she stopped. She understood the sanctity of a woman's kitchen from how her Mom had felt about hers.

"Well, good morning. Look at this. I didn't expect the help, but I sure do appreciate it!"

Mildred smiled at the recognition of her unsolicited efforts. "Good morning. What more can I do, now?" Together they arranged the meal, Lena giving directions with Mildred as her willing assistant.

"Good morning, Mr. Olson. May I pour you coffee?" He accepted the greeting and returned her smile. The three sat down to eat. Charles spoke first.

"Here at home, we're Charles and Lena. If we're outside, Mr. and Mrs. Olson are best. We talked, and you're welcome to stay here with us for now. We'll see if that works out. Lena and I have no children of our own. Now, you're not a child, but I mean we're used to just ourselves in the house. We'll have to see if your being here works for everybody. Fair enough?"

"Yes, thank you." Overwhelmed by the kindness of three strangers, her throat thickened.

Lena turned, leaned over and put her arm around the shaking shoulders. Her hand cupped the girl's shoulder until the tremors subsided.

"After we do the breakfast dishes, we've got a full day ahead."

"Yes, ma'am."

"I'm going to introduce you to the other friend Mr. McBride mentioned in his letter. That's Florence, who owns the Café over across the way. After that, I have a job in my store for you. We'll go back to the store and if you like the offer, I'll get you started. If you take the job, you'll have a 'store account', so you can get anything you need, put it on a list, and I'll take it out of your weekly check."

"Yes, that is a full day, but it sounds wonderful. Thanks."

* * * *

The morning chores done and Charles off to work, they descended the outside stairs. At the bottom, an asphalt-paved street fronted the store. A chicken-wire-enclosed yard was on the side. A chipped white ceramic bowl full of eggs sat on the bottom step. Mildred picked up the bowl and offered it to Lena, who took the eggs and gestured to continue over to the Mercantile's doorway. There she set the dish down next to the door.

"That little house is where Pat lived. He shared it with Duano Lagomarsino. Eggs were not rationed, so the boys began keeping chickens: eggs for themselves and the occasional stewing hen. As their flock grew, they had more eggs than they could use, so I'd take the extras for the store to sell." Lena pointed to the adjoining side yard.

Inside the fenced yard a flock of chickens busily pecked at unseen targets or clustered in small groups. A wooden chicken coop with a door at one end and a chicken-sized door with its own wooden ramp sat in one corner of the yard. The scent of manure wafted over the women as it rode the breeze off Liberty Bay.

"Duano gathers the eggs every morning before he heads off to work at the Keyport station. My husband is the Chief of Security there." She swung her hand over to point at the front gate with its guard stations.

"After work in the evenings, Mr. Lagomarsino feeds his flock and cleans the coop, so you'll see him later today. He's too old for you, but that doesn't make him any less handsome." Her voice shifted to a conspiratorial whisper.

"A girl who came into the store told me he's hornier than a two-peckered Billy goat." Lena's hand reached up to cover her mouth, "I can't believe I said that out loud."

Mildred laughed and laughed. When she regained her composure she added, "Excuse me." Mrs. Olson had a very human sense of humor.

Lena pointed across the street to Smith's Café, and they walked over. Summoned by the tinkle of the bell high on the inside of the door, Florence Mitchell emerged from the kitchen, brushing flour off her hands.

"Howdy, Lena," came her customary greeting. "And howdy to you too." Florence extended a flour-covered hand to Mildred. "Coffee, ladies? And the other smell is a hot coffee cake. We should probably sample that."

"Yes to both, if you can join us for a minute while I introduce my new assistant. This is Mildred."

"Take a seat and I'll be right back with coffee and cake." Glancing at Mildred, Florence asked, "How many coffees?" Lena looked over, encouraging Mildred to answer for herself. Mildred's greatest fear was questions about her past. Whatever she said now could come back to haunt her later. Only being asked about coffee came as a relief.

"Coffee please. Cream and sugar."

With a confirming nod, Florence moved off as the two took their seats.

Back from the kitchen, she off-loaded her round tray, placing coffee and steaming cake at three places, and milk and sugar within Mildred's easy reach.

The girl doctored her coffee with as much milk and sugar as fit.

Lena slid Pat's letter across the table. After a quick read, Florence passed it back and winked at Lena.

"So how old are you?" asked Florence as she smiled.

"Eighteen," was Mildred's first answer.

"How old really?" Florence asked again with the same smile and a closer lean.

"Seventeen..."

This time both women leaned forward.

"At my next birthday anyway," Mildred reluctantly admitted.

Satisfied the final answer matched the girl, both women leaned back and shared knowing winks.

"I have an Aunt Mildred in San Jose," offered Florence. "Mildred is an old English name. It means 'great strength.' Do you like Mildred? Or maybe have you thought about something more modern, like Millie?"

"Oh, I like Millie. Yes, please call me Millie. I like having a new name to start a new chapter to my life. I'm not just a country girl anymore. I'm almost," pointing in the general direction of Seattle, "a big city girl."

"Well, Millie it is," smiled Florence.

Lena gave a confirming nod.

"I'm talking too much; our coffee cake will get cold," announced Florence. Three forks rose in response.

When Dan, the postmaster, strode in at ten A.M., Florence introduced Millie, emphasizing the connection to Pat McBride and her soon-to-begin job in the Olsons' store.

Each introduction boosted a sense of genuine acceptance. Mildred saw herself as Millie now, unshackled from her bleak past. This was her chance to never be used or abused again. Of this she was certain. The new name signified the willingness of these people in Keyport to accept her for who she wanted to be, here and now.

After coffee and introductions, they walked back across the street to the Mercantile. A breeze off Liberty Bay carried strange odors to her nose. It was the smell of seaweed at low tide, baking in the sun, uncovered by the waters of the bay. As they crossed the covered wood porch of the Mercantile, Millie picked up the bowl of eggs and stepped aside while Lena opened the door and turned on the overhead lights.

"Millie, you can be my shop girl and clerk. I will pay you $10 a week plus your room and board. Does that sound all right to you?"

It seemed fair, if not outright generous. The shelter and support here far exceeded anything she'd received before in her entire life.

"It does, and thank you for the opportunity."

Millie knew she could do what needed to be done. Hard work and self-reliance were her strengths, not her problems. But her distrust of men needed to be put aside somehow. Keyport looked like a place where she'd have to trust strangers to succeed. This leap of faith did seem possible, since all she'd seen so far was the collective willingness of strangers to trust her and, of course, to trust Pat McBride's judgement.

"OK, here's what we'll do. You'll learn where things go by doing small jobs for me. Ask me questions as I explain things or later when you think of something while you're working. When you finish a job, let me know. I'll check what you did, and we'll go on from there. Sound fine?"

Millie showed her agreement with a smile.

"To help you get settled, you now have your own store charge account. Any things you need, like girl stuff, set aside over behind our cash register." Lena motioned toward the ornate brass National cash register sitting on a countertop across the store.

"We'll keep a list of what you take, and I'll adjust your first week's pay. The important thing is for you to get essentials: a second dress, shoes maybe. That's up to you.

"Okay so let's get you started. First, we'll do today's eggs. I want you to make sure each egg is clean, carrying nothing else that the chicken laid. There's a sink in the back, if any of them need washing." Lena pointed towards the curtain separating the front of the shop from the storeroom.

"Put the clean eggs in one of the cardboard egg boxes over in the corner behind the counter. Tell me how many eggs we have, and I'll enter them as a credit for Duano in our ledger. Rinse out the bowl and put it back out on the stairs where you found it this morning."

"Let's see, what else do I need to tell you before we start our day," and she paused. "No matter, follow me. I'll show you where we hang up our coats, the bathroom and the coffee pot."

* * * *

After dinner that evening Mildred — now Millie—retired for the night. Charles and Lena sat at the kitchen table. Over a final cup of coffee Lena shared with him what had filled her day.

"Florence and I had coffee with her this morning. It was really coffee and questions both. She met Dan, too, and we had a good day in the store getting her oriented. Mildred is sixteen at the moment. She followed my directions and did fine with each little job. When she finished one job, she'd come to me and ask for more work, so she's not lazy."

Charles listened attentively and sipped his coffee with an approving nod. "Tomorrow I'll start putting out inquiries to law enforcement in Oregon and Northern California. We need to make sure our young guest is neither a fugitive nor a runaway."

* * * *

The next morning, Millie made her usual point of being first in the kitchen. Table set and coffee brewing, she crossed through the parlor to glimpse Duano, perhaps. Did he know the truth about her back story? Would her simple answers, unchallenged by the Olsons, also satisfy him? Worse yet for her peace of mind was the possibility any day a letter to the Olsons put her at risk of being exposed for the whore she'd been.

The flat gray sky begrudgingly allowed light into the parlor. But there he was, in with the chickens, wearing a canvas coat over blue coveralls. The short bill of a khaki cap blocked her view of his face as Duano closed the henhouse door, the same chipped ceramic bowl cradled in one hand. Millie watched as he crossed the yard to the foot of the Olsons' stairs. He set the bowlful of brown eggs on the bottom step where it had rested yesterday morning. Taking three eggs out, he nestled them in his hand and walked back across the yard and into his side door.

Breakfast, she imagined during her walk back to the kitchen.

* * * *

It took a week for Charles's requests for his 12 records checks on Mildred Mercer to come back. She was not a fugitive, a runaway nor reported missing. That ended Millie's second week in Keyport on a high note.

4. A New Friend

As days became weeks, Millie saw the handsome neighbor daily, but always from a distance. She liked what she saw. By now he must have seen her. That he had not approached her, at first a relief, began to seem something else. But what? A snub? Disdain, because he knew the truth about her? She had to know.

Millie began watching and trying to discern patterns in Duano's routine. Did he stop for coffee at Smith's regularly or go out for breakfast on his days off? Was the ferry pier his hang-out? Did he fish, smoke, or drink a beer there? Should she contrive a chance encounter? *No, better to wait for him to come into the Mercantile.*

The opportunity came on the Friday of her third week in Keyport. A small silver bell on a metal bracket by the top of the Mercantile's door rang as the door swung open. Millie looked up from her chore, the daily cleaning of the tops of the glass display cases. It was him. Lena was in the back, so her moment was now. A spray bottle of glass cleaner and a wad of crumpled paper were her only armaments as Duano sauntered across the store. He began pulling cans: stew, hash, canned peaches, pasta, until they filled the crook of his arm. Balancing them, he walked to where she worked at the counter.

The words and plans practiced in Millie's head were gone. Even if she appeared a beautiful, willowy 17-year-old, inside were the same fears she'd suffered when Miss Della had taken her as a new addition to her livestock. Tongue-tied by the proximity of her handsome neighbor, she'd lost her chance to use her well-rehearsed lines.

With a clatter, his armload of cans dropped in front of Millie, inches from her hands that still clutched the cleaning supplies.

"I'm not done but you can start tallying my bill." Next he moved to the produce bins. He examined and selected half a dozen red potatoes and an equal number of yellow onions. Cradling the vegetables between forearm and torso, Duano leaned over and moved his arm away from his chest. His cargo dropped to the glass top and bounced. Onions and spuds rolled, and three escapees hit the floor.

"Shit!" The epithet escaped Duano's lips. He gave the young clerk a quick glance.

She tried not to react.

"Excuse me." Then he went down on one knee to retrieve the produce. As he stood up, onions in hand, Millie smiled.

He returned her smile and resumed shopping. He came back with his final items—coffee, sugar, salt—and placed them on the counter. She had the bill underway and had placed his first two armloads in a cardboard box. She added the last items to the tab, placing each in the box after listing it.

She looked up the neighbor's 'egg credit' and listed it below the total cost of his purchases. Duano didn't check the bill but slid it back, all the while holding eye contact. He drew his wallet from one trouser pocket and a quarter from another. He took out three, one-dollar bills and placed them on the counter, then put the coin down, covering George Washington's picture.

Then he gave her an appraising look. He smiled but didn't speak as he held Millie in his gaze. He was still staring and smiling when she slid his money off the countertop and put it in the cash register.

For all her skills in seducing men, Millie wasn't yet ready for a man who neither grabbed nor groped her. She was more alarmed by her apparent lack of effect on the male stranger than by his fixed gaze. Long ago at Madam Della's she'd overcome her initial fear of men and her own feeling of powerlessness. Men paid for the pleasure of her body, and that gave her a measure of control. She wanted some control now, yearned for it. But a handsome, strong, polite, and non-exploitive male was both a mystery and a challenge.

Millie watched as Duano picked up the grocery box. Cradling it in one strong arm, he turned and left. Free at last from her own paralysis, she stepped over to the full-length mirror in the store. She'd yearned for, dreamed about and planned their initial meeting. In her dreams she'd be both witty and irresistible. But that hadn't happened; she'd frozen, and he'd not shown even a glimpse of interest. Why? Gazing at her reflection she checked herself, but for what? *A bit of cereal stuck to a front tooth? Is something dangling from a nostril? Why didn't he even ask my name?*

* * * *

The recognition Millie wanted from Duano Lagomarsino finally came two weeks later, in the Olsons' vegetable garden across from his chickens.

Months of Lena's cooking and nights of uninterrupted sleep had changed Millie's appearance from a too-slim teen into an attractive young woman. She filled out her flannel in an unmistakably female way. Her hair was returned to its natural red, and she kept it tied back with a checked bandana. What had once been Charlie Olson's khaki work pants were now her baggy shorts. They were too big in the waist by half, so a well-used leather belt bunched the shorts at her middle. But the shorts couldn't hide the shapely hips she now possessed. Soiled white cotton gloves covered Millie's hands as she hoed weeds from between the rows of the summer garden.

She noticed Duano as he went from house to coop and returned to his house with a basket of eggs. *If he'll ignore me, I'll ignore him right back.*

Duano returned to the yard with a galvanized bucket in his hand. Millie expected the daily feeding of the flock was about to happen. It didn't.

With an occasional glance from the corner of her eye, she watched as he went into the chicken coop, taking along a flat scoop shovel which usually leaned against an outside wall. When he came out, he set the bucket down and returned the shovel to its former place. Taking an armload of straw from a bale in the back of the yard he reentered the coop, only to return a few minutes later. He picked up the bucket by its wire handle and walked to the low fence that separated the yards. When he stopped, a broad grin was on his face.

When she didn't stop hoeing or otherwise acknowledge his presence, he called out, "Hey, you in the baggy pants."

Millie rested the blade of the hoe next to her bare feet. Leaning on the long handle, she turned to face the speaker.

"This is for you," and he held up the bucket.

Expressionless, Millie walked towards the fence. From two feet away, the smell of ammonia wafted up to assault her nose.

"Chicken manure. How nice. You sure know how to impress a girl," she grinned.

"It's for your garden and will do wonders for the plants. I've got to clean the coop anyway, so it's yours if you want it. I know it doesn't smell like roses."

41

"I'm a farm girl. I know all about that stuff."

Millie was no longer the scared teen who'd arrived in Keyport four months before. The confidence needed to run away from home in Madras, Oregon and run again from Madam Della's brothel had returned.

* * * *

Duano started their courtship by asking Millie to help him plant a small garden in a corner of the chicken yard. His hens kept bugs out of the garden. Duano used the first harvest of Swiss chard and garlic to recreate a favorite dish from his childhood. Sharing the preparation, serving and eating of the meal impressed her. Here was a guy who could take care of himself. He wasn't looking for a maid or Mommy. Best of all, he liked to talk and share activities. What stood out about him most was how he gave her his time and never tried to impress or buy her with trinkets.

They fished together at the end of the ferry pier. Millie scaled and cleaned their catch of ocean perch, and Duano cooked them. They both liked the movies that came to the theater in the neighboring town of Poulsbo. Cards became a favorite shared activity, and they learned each other's favorite games. Best of all, they shared a love for each other's company.

He took pains not to push a physical side to their budding relationship. At age seventeen, seven years his junior, Millie was now in the full flower of womanhood. She began to wonder, even worry that she might not be attractive to him. *What a waste for us both that would be.*

In late spring of 1945, after Duano fixed dinner in his kitchen, they first shared one another. Millie offered her hand across the tabletop and rose as he took it in his own. He pulled her around the table and into his arms. Nothing was said as they hugged, her head leaning on his chest. His grasp engulfed her, and he leaned in for a kiss. Millie raised her mouth to his ear. Three words passed her lips, "Yes—now—please." Not another word was spoken while he carried her to his bed.

Two hours later, as they lay side by side, they spoke another three magic words as they embraced. First from her lips and then from his came, "I love you."

When Millie dressed and returned to the Olsons', it was full dark as she came up the outside stairs and into the living room. Lena greeted her with a smile.

"How was dinner?"

"It was wonderful. He cooks for me." Millie spoke with an uncommon grin radiating across her face.

"Yes, I can see you enjoyed the evening" Lena said with what Millie thought might be a too-knowing look.

"And after dinner?"

"We tried a new game."

"What's it called?"

"Hearts."

"Charlie taught me that game years ago. We still play it sometimes, but not as much as we used too." Silence followed between the two until Lena finally broke it.

"Hon, it's a wonderful game, if you find the right partner," and she gave Millie's hand one quick squeeze as she stood. "Well, we both have to work tomorrow. I'll see you at breakfast."

5. Keyport, August 15, 1945

V-J Day came with as much exuberance as the anger December 7th had brought. As word spread between buildings, men shut off their machines. Everyone from shops, offices and guard shacks found their way outside to the streets, cheering and congratulating each other.

The noise of the crowd combined with a cacophony of boat whistles from ferries on Puget Sound and ships in the harbor. Car horns blared. A roar from across the water in Seattle joined in a background symphony of joy.

Outside the small station chapel, a quieter crowd gathered. Friends, coworkers and strangers, led by the Keyport Station Commander, clasped hands. They thanked God for the deliverance of their country. They said a prayer for the servicemen who would come home and for those who wouldn't be returning.

Lena and Millie left the store and began running towards the Main Gate. Marine guards seemed uncaring, as the gates were opened to the streams of civilians and workers coming and going. Lena's destination was Charlie's office in Building #1. Millie had never been on the station, so she stopped at the gate, hoping to greet Duano as he headed home.

Duano's progress through the crowds was slow. He shared congratulations and back-slaps with coworkers and others, some of whom had been strangers until now. Everyone was united in the collective 'us' that had won a world war. They had all helped in achieving today's victory!

Making his way through the throng up the hill towards the Main Gate, he caught sight of Millie. As their eyes met, she waved and ran towards her lover, who met her with open arms. He lifted Millie and spun her around. The crowd parted as her legs left the ground and splayed out behind in a widening arc. They kissed and kissed again as the mass of celebrants swirled around them. When the crowd thinned enough to allow passage, they walked back arm in arm towards the Mercantile.

Duano and Millie sat together on the front porch of the store and watched the continuing celebration. The store had been untouched by the crowd. Across the street, Florence was standing in front of her café, Postmaster Dan and Artie, the fry cook, by her side. The noise of the celebration began to diminish and finally dropped to a level where words not spoken directly into an ear could be heard.

Millie's wrist curled around Duano's forearm as they sat side by side on the porch. Turning his torso away from the crowd he put a hand over hers. "All I know is I'm so Goddamn glad it's over." He paused, "and I love you. Will you marry me?" The question hung there unanswered as she searched his face for confirmation of his sincerity.

"I'll ask again from my knees if that helps?"

First came Millie's smile, and then she hugged him before giving her answer. "Yes, oh yes, I'll marry you." With that Duano went silent as he took her head in his big hands. He kissed her smiling lips.

Then with a note of panic in his voice he asked, "Is the store open?"

Unsure of what was in her lover's mind Millie answered. "Yes. We just closed the door and left when we heard the news."

"I need to make two quick purchases. Can I go inside?"

"Sure."

"I'll be back." Inside the Mercantile, Duano knew where he was going but first he put a $5 bill on the countertop. He picked up a single White Owl Corona cigar and put it in his shirt pocket. From a stack at the corner of one counter he hoisted up a wooden case of quart bottles of Rainier beer. With the beer resting on one arm, he returned to the porch and set the case behind their seat. He slid the cigar band off the Corona and placed it on the third finger of Millie's left hand.

"This will have to do for your engagement ring. I was too afraid to buy one."

"This is the first thing you've ever given me." Then leaning forward and lowering her voice she added, "Except what you give me in bed." That reference to a shared secret brought smiles to both their faces. Millie looked at the cigar-band ring. "It's beautiful."

Raising a hand to signal 'wait,' Duano turned and grabbed two bottles of beer from the wood box. "An engagement toast to us," but again he paused, setting the beers down on the porch.

"I'll be right back." With no further explanation he got up and trotted across the street to Smith's and spoke to Florence. Nodding, she went inside, returning with two glasses and handing them to him before he hurried back.

"You don't need to drink from a bottle when you're with me." He gave her a glass. Picking up one of the quart bottles, he popped off the cap with the opener secured to his key chain. "To us; thank you for saying yes."

* * * *

Duano got the expected news in April 1946. Keyport was downsizing now that the war was won. The reduced need for torpedoes meant layoffs were coming. Because of his good work at the station, he was offered other government jobs.

Duano received a list of options. Ammunition plants in Texas and Oklahoma; Military Depots in northern California, central Washington or Arkansas. Closer to his former home were shipyards in Philly or near Chicago. Filling out the list of job openings were Army and Army Air Corps bases. He could go to the naval base in Bremerton or a naval research station at Bayview, Idaho. There were lots of possibilities to consider.

Being engaged to marry meant the choice was not his alone. Duano saw an opportunity to get closer to home. Fort Dix had openings. He did his thinking out loud so his future bride wasn't left out of the choice.

Together Duano and Millie reached out to Charles and Lena for advice. Across the Olsons' kitchen table the four batted around the choices. She wanted to stay in the Northwest. Duano desired the Northeast.

Charles shared what he knew about the choices which made each of their short-lists. As Chief of Security at Keyport, he knew Duano's security clearance gave him access to better options. Olson also volunteered to write his friend a letter of recommendation.

Taking into account what they had learned from Charles, Duano called home for a private conversation with his father, Primo Lagomarsino. Father and son reviewed the list. He was surprised when his father recommended an option on Millie's list: Bayview, Idaho.

"Pop, why Idaho? I don't get it."

"Our family has used north Idaho for a long time. Every so often, someone might need to cool off for a while. We've stashed people at Spirit Lake, or sometimes in Spirit Lake, when things got too hot for them in Jersey.

Your being out there might be a good thing." Primo was silent for a moment, before adding, "For family business. You understand?"

"Like when you sent Uncle Luigi on that vacation."

"Like that. We have a connection to a restaurant in Coeur d' Alene, 30 miles south of Spirit Lake. If you and your girl make it to Bayview, go to Luigi's in Coeur d' Alene. It's on the lakeshore just east of the town. Tell Luigi I sent you. Out there he mostly goes by Brizz instead of Brizzalerra.

Duano shared his father's recommendation with Millie, but not Primo's reasons. Their choice made, he put a question to her. "Will you come with me now, before we're married? We'll make a place together."

"And get married. I'm not going to be your shack mouse."

"Absolutely, soon as we get settled, we'll get married. You are never going to be *just* a shack mouse." He hit the word 'just' hard for emphasis. "You are everything to me always, babe."

With the marriage question settled, he applied for the job at the Naval Underwater Research Station in Bayview, Idaho. Two days later his application for the supply warehouse manager position went in. A letter of recommendation from Charles Olson to his counterpart at Bayview accompanied the application. Two weeks later, Duano got the job.

He shared the good news with the Olsons. Duano's final day at Keyport would be in another two weeks. Until then, his fiancé stayed with them. The pair's last two weeks at Keyport were filled with goodbyes and paperwork. Millie focused on acquiring the basics of a kitchen. Duano focused on getting them a car. Their suitcases, boxes of pots and pans, towels and bedding filled the black 1940 Ford coupe he bought.

At the ferry dock, Florence, Dan, the Olsons, and a cadre of friends from Keyport waved goodbye. From the back of the Black Ball Ferry car deck, the new couple waved goodbye to Keyport.

6. Bayview, Idaho, May 1946

The transit from Keyport to Bayview and Duano's new job took them two days. When they passed through Coeur d' Alene, Idaho, the blue of the water drew them to the shore. The beauty of the lake and the huge forests descending to the shoreline were new to them. The air was full of the smell of pines and sounds of machinery from the numerous lumber mills along the shore.

They watched tugs on the lake pushing rafts of logs. The steady low rumble of the tugs belied the great size of the rafts. Hand in hand the weary travelers ran to the water's edge. They dropped their shoes and socks on the hard-packed silt of the beach. Hand in hand again the two waded knee-deep into the icy shallows of the lake. There they stood for long moments devouring the vistas of forest and water. Millie began waving her arms as a tug passed close. Duano joined in her excitement by pumping his right arm in a signal to the tug's captain. Three long blasts answered from the tug's steam whistle.

Duano and Millie sat on a large driftwood log behind the beach. Using his socks as improvised towels they dried their feet and brushed off the mica-flecked silt. Back in the Ford coupe the couple drove through the quiet streets of town and on north.

After skirting the town of Hayden, they began to see signs along the roadside. "Farragut Naval Training Base, Eight Miles." As the distance numbers decreased, roadside signage increased. 'Payday loans," "Cars—Nothing down for those who serve." At last a sign pointed them toward a two-lane road; "Camp Farragut, 1 mile." Under the trees along the road to Farragut lay a thin blanket of snow.

Millie had a road map showing in more detail their location in Idaho's Panhandle. Bayview was just east of the Farragut Naval Training Station, which they'd be passing through. The Main Gate and guard shack were now just ahead.

"Babe, hand me my orders from the glove box." Duano stopped at the shack. A red-and-white-striped boom blocked entry to the camp. She passed him the requested paperwork as he rolled down the car window.

"Good morning," he said to the two navy guards who'd emerged from the shack.

"Good morning," answered one of the two. "Where are you headed?"

Duano handed over his transfer papers for Bayview.

One guard began examining the documents while his companion circled the car. Nothing suspicious was noticed in the paperwork or vehicle and his papers were returned.

"Keep going straight. A mile up ahead the road forks. Keep straight and Bayview is at the bottom of the hill. You can't miss it. Park in the lot next to the guard shack. You'll need to go inside the shack to check in and get on-base directions. That place does 'secret' stuff, so I can't help you any further. Welcome to Idaho," and with a nod the navy guards returned to the warmth of their post.

The Naval Training Base was still turning out new sailors. They saw rows of barracks, drill fields and a parade ground as they passed through. They descended the hill, and another huge lake emerged through the curtain of tall red cedar and larch trees.

"What lake is this?" Millie asked.

"This one is Lake Pend Oreille. Sounds French to me, but I've got no idea what it means."

Rounding the final curve, they approached the Bayview guard shack. Duano pulled the Ford into the small gravel parking lot alongside a tall wire fence crowned with coils of barbed wire. "Babe, you wait here while I go inside."

The square, cement gate-control office had tinted windows. After ascending two steps Duano entered the office. Three men in naval uniforms worked behind a counter that divided the office.

"Can I help you?" The speaker came up to Duano as he took out his transfer papers and laid them on the counter.

"I'm transferring in from Keyport. I'm the new supply warehouse manager. My wife is outside in our car."

The clerk examined the papers on the counter.

"I'll call your boss, Master Chief Norris, and let him know you're here. He'll get you settled in. Welcome aboard."

"Any idea how long it will be for him to come over? It gets cold in the car for her."

"There's a canteen on station. I'll let you drive in and the Master Chief can meet you there. It's warm and they serve simple meals, so you can get coffee, a Coke or a sandwich while you wait. You OK with that?"

Duano replied with a "Yes."

"I'll let you through the gate and you'll be driving only a block. You'll see the canteen on your right."

They shook hands and Duano walked back to his car. They drove through the opened gate, parked, and went into the canteen.

Master Chief Norris found the two having coffee. Duano passed his transfer papers and Charles Olson's letter to Norris, who read the praise contained therein.

"Welcome aboard."

Norris got his own coffee and returned to their table doing a quiet 'size-up' of the two recent transplants. As they discussed the trip from Keyport and Duano's previous duties, Norris's concerns seemed to vanish. The letter from his counterpart at Keyport satisfied him that the supervisory job had gone to the right man.

Turning his attention to Millie, Norris asked, "I hope you'll like our small circle of friends. I know you'll want to get settled. I bet you have preferences for your home."

She smiled but didn't speak. Norris continued now, addressing them both.

"Since we knew you were coming, your quarters are clean and vacant. You folks can move right in if you like the place. After coffee, we can walk over for your inspection. We keep our senior people close, so the house is right outside our Main Gate. If you don't like it, no problem. Our housing services clerk will help you find something of your choosing."

"It sounds fine to me." Duano then turning to Millie, "Does that sound OK to you, babe?"

She squeezed his fingers, smiled, and replied, "I'm excited. Let's go see the place." Hand in hand, they fell in behind Norris.

The Master Chief walked them back towards the Main Gate leading off the station. Fifty yards away was the town of Bayview. On the right was a row of modest wood-framed houses, some with fenced yards, others not. Norris stopped at the fourth house.

"Here we are." He held the door open as the new transfers entered. "The previous tenant left some well-used furniture. It's yours if you want it. You folks do your walk around. I'll wait here in the living room."

The 1,000 square foot house contained a living room, two bedrooms, a single bath, and a rectangular combination kitchen and eating area. Millie began checking each cabinet and cupboard for telltale mouse droppings or roaches and found none. In the kitchen, they stood transfixed by the lake view out through the rear-facing windows. There, across the gentle slope of the back yard, lay an arm of Lake Pend Oreille. Tall green timber bordered the shocking blue of the water for as far as they could see.

Master Chief Norris turned when he heard them walk in. "What do you think?"

"How much per month?" Duano asked.

"$30.00 and that's a subsidized rate for station personnel." Norris added, "Utilities included."

"Millie, shall we take this place?" She answered with a smile and a nod. "We'll take it," came from both their lips.

Norris then launched into a short list of details: garbage collection, and access to the Farragut commissary and exchange. Then he passed over two sets of house keys.

With the house inspection complete, the three continued a walking tour of the town. To the left on a gentle slope was a city park, complete with a flagpole and gazebo. Farther down, a post office, diner, and gas station came into view. Across the street were a bait shop, a bar, and a combination grocery and dry goods store. Three more blocks of paved streets took them to the far edge of town where it bordered National Forest land. The tour concluded, Norris spoke again as they walked back toward the research station.

"Mrs. Lagomarsino, I'll take your husband back with me and get your car access through the gate. Would you mind if I borrowed him for another hour? I want to show him our headquarters building and my office."

"That's fine. I'll wait at our new house. When the car shows up, I can unpack and begin assembling my household."

"I'll have someone bring your car over," Norris said.

Millie left unsaid any explanation of their marital status. Adultery was a crime. With the war over, both feared that a rigid, moralistic tone might return to the country. All bets were off during the war, but the proverbial party was now at an end.

Duano and Norris proceeded to the station's headquarters for his photo ID and then on to Finance. "You'll need to accompany your wife here for her photo ID," Norris advised. At Finance, Duano opted to have the rent on their house deducted from his bi-monthly check. By five o'clock his in-processing was complete. He walked the scant 100 yards out the gate to his new home.

* * * *

On Duano's first full day at work, Master Chief Norris took him on a walking tour of the station. "You came from Keyport, I understand." Norris explained Bayview's mission and how it figured in the national defense strategy. Like Keyport, Bayview had a fixed security post and roving patrols. A security fence enclosed the landward side of the entire station. As yet, Duano couldn't tell what the undersea research station did, but whatever it was, it was secret. Set out from the lakefront was a series of floating docks and piers, each accessed by a gangplank to the lakeshore.

"Since you're a supervisor, you'll get a photo ID that allows you to enter all areas of the station. Your wife is eligible for her own ID, but with limited access. Where Keyport was a production facility, we do research here, important research. The torpedoes Keyport produced went aboard the boats we designed and tested. Our job is to make bigger, faster and quieter subs."

"We know about the Balao class subs that replaced the Gato boats," Duano commented. "They were what, a hundred feet longer? My old roommate, Pat McBride, told me about the Balaos. He'd been a machinist working on the old Mark 14 steam torpedoes. When Newport reverse engineered a recovered German electric torpedo, we switched our production to the Mark 18 electrics. Pat transferred to Mare Island. He's now a lead man installing the four diesels in each boat and tuning them to work together."

"Yup, the Balaos are bigger, faster and quieter. That was our first design that's now in production. Getting those 5,000 horses to work together as one quiet unit was a big part of our research. If the enemy can't hear us, he can't find us."

They passed a floating dock tethered parallel to the beach. A short gangplank connected dock and beach. "I'll show you something," and Norris strode over the short ramp and stepped onto the dock. Duano followed but stopped after his first three steps on the ramp.

Transfixed by the clarity of the lake and the variegated tones of the rocky bottom, Duano knelt. He reached into the crystal-clear water and leaned down, trying to grasp a single pebble. The stone was beyond his reach. "How deep is it here? I wanted to pick up a pebble as a souvenir for Millie."

Chief Norris stepped back and pointed into the lake water. "The pebbles you see are actually boulders. The water beneath us is 100 feet deep here in Scenic Bay."

"No shit?"

"No shit." Pointing off to their right, "In the middle, the lake is over 1100 feet deep, and the water is still. Nothing flows into Lake Pend Oreille at this end, so the water is quiet. That's what we want for acoustic testing. Pure, quiet water, so we can discern sounds from the boat away from natural sounds of the ocean. So, what we do here is very secret.

"Our hull designs have gone into production and those boats are now in service. We've also created the Barracuda and Tang class boats. At the moment our new baby is the Albacore class, which should be approved and go into production next spring.

"You'll hear what I'm about to tell you again, when you get your ID badge. What we do here is Top Secret. If anyone asks what you do here, your answer is, 'I didn't say what I did, just that I work there.'"

Duano's duty station was a warehouse at the south end of the compound. Inside he saw rows of five-tier-high steel racks. Between the rows were wide aisles. An electric forklift disappeared along an aisle off to their right. Norris led the way to one of two freestanding rooms inside the warehouse enclosure. In the first room was a wall of gray metal file cabinets. A single desk and swivel chair completed the furnishings.

"That's your desk. The cabinets contain shipping and receiving documents for the contents of the warehouse. Those racks we saw have everything needed to assemble a one-quarter scale test submarine. A unique number identifies every part." Over at the desk, Norris put his hand on a wooden in-box.

"Orders come in from the different research sections: hull design, propulsion, acoustic material. Your crew fills the orders. When the order is complete, your shop will deliver the goods to the requesting team."

"That's all I have to do?" Duano smiled as they left the office.

"That's it, just track on-hand supply for 11,000 items worth over $10,000,000. Fill and deliver orders. Easy." They stepped inside the second room. Metal lockers lined two walls; wooden benches ran parallel to the lockers. He could see lavatories and showers through a door off to their right.

"Find yourself an empty locker. Since V-J Day we're back to one shift, 7A.M. to 4P.M. five days per week. If you need more time, you have authority to ask for volunteers and pay overtime; just no overtime pay for yourself. If you work more, you get compensatory leave. Your crew is all War Department civilians. As the boss, your work-day hours are up to you. But I suggest two things. Empty your in-box daily. Never let an order go out until you have personally checked the request against the completed shipment."

Duano remained silent during Norris's narrative until now.

"I understand. My day begins before my crew's and ends when the work is finished. Not at 4 o'clock. No problem." He was wondering what he'd gotten himself into. But he'd not give voice to any doubts to Norris, Millie, or anyone else.

* * * *

While Duano handled his on-post issues, Millie had her own list. Now the real process of settling in began. She delighted in setting up her own first house. The furniture left inside was not fancy, but it was serviceable and clean. High on her shopping list were a welcome mat, new curtains, new sheets, and a vase or two for the fresh flowers she hoped to grow. The list included toilet paper, curtain fabric, food for dinner, and wall decorations. With their car unpacked and her kitchen basics dealt with, she turned to putting away clothes in the single dresser and closet.

Her unpacking now done, Millie left a note for Duano, "Gone exploring." Neither of them knew how long his first day on the job would be.

From her new front porch, Millie surveyed the town. The buildings inched up a gradual slope moving inland from the lakeshore. She counted rooftops on the three ascending streets, and three more which fanned out from left to right.

The dry goods store in the heart of town was a place to start. Duano saw to it that she was never without pocket money, so off to the store she went. She might find some of the items on her list. If not she'd be able to tell him what was there.

May days were growing longer. It wouldn't be twilight until 7:30 and not full dark until after 8:00. Millie passed the Post Office, a one-pump combination Richfield gas station/garage, the 'Angler's Bait Shop' and the 'No Reservations' Tavern.

The unpainted, covered wood porch at the store was a single step above the pavement. "Dry Goods" read the wooden sign hanging from the porch eaves. No store name, nothing more. A bell rang when Millie opened the door and stepped inside. The single big room was well lit by a row of windows above the porch cover. She was doing a slow visual inventory when a woman's voice floated out from the back of the store.

"Hello, can I help you? I'm Bonnie, and this is my little place. Welcome."

"Hello, we just arrived. I'm exploring the town and shopping for things we need. Do you folks carry curtain fabric or linens? I need sheets, pillowcases, and a spread for our double bed. Oh, I almost forgot, and toilet paper."

"You came to the right place."

Millie surveyed the canned food and produce options. "My husband and I came from a small town over on the Washington coast and now he's working at Bayview. It's kind of hard leaving friends and making new ones in a new town."

"Been there, done that. My Royce and I moved here from a big city. Fortunately for us, we already had one family of close friends here. That helped a lot. I have to tell you, just from our little conversation today, making friends won't be a problem for you. How do I know that? Well you've already made your first friend." Bonnie smiled and gave Millie a quick hug. "Welcome to Bayview."

Millie mentioned which house was theirs and discovered that Bonnie and her husband Royce were their neighbors. Royce had transferred from defense work with Lockheed Aviation in Southern California. The neighbors on the left were Curtis, Betty, and their young son David.

Goods in hand and starting to feel connected to the town, Millie headed back to christen her kitchen with a home-cooked meal. Duano found her already at work when he walked in.

Over dinner that night, Millie told him about her visit to the store. "Bonnie, our next-door neighbor, works there. She told me about the other neighbors and about another little town, Athol, not far away. I need to learn to drive. Will you teach me? Pretty as Bayview is, I don't want to be stuck here in the winter when it's too cold to be outside."

"Athol. It sounds like it was named by somebody with a harelip."

As they shared a simple dinner, Millie put down her fork, and fixed her gaze on him. "Are you still going to marry me?"

Setting down his utensils, he reached across the table and took her hand.

"Yes I am. I tell you what; we'll start looking for a church or chapel this weekend. I think we can find a minister in Coeur d' Alene. How does that sound?"

Thus reassured, Millie smiled and squeezed his hand.

7. A Wedding

As promised, on the couple's first weekend in North Idaho they drove into Coeur d' Alene, the nearest city. Not knowing where to go to get married, they cruised the city, exploring. Government Way, a tree-lined boulevard with a wide center strip of trees and lawn, led them toward the downtown. There they found 'The Hitching Post Wedding Chapel.'

"Let's see what we've got here," Duano said.

"Yes," Millie replied with a big smile. They parked and entered the little building.

Ida Dodge met the two inside. "Welcome to our chapel. My, but you two are a lovely couple. We would love to have the honor of getting you married up. My husband, the minister, is available."

She pointed to a small framed menu on an adjacent wall. "We've got flowers, a modest selection of rings, even music if you folks want. We also have pre-approved marriage license forms, if you folks don't already have your license."

Duano looked over at Millie's big smile and spoke up. "That's what we're here for, so let's get it done."

"Johnny! Get out here! We have guests who want you to tie the knot for them." She asked Millie, "Flowers, darling?"

But Duano spoke first. "Let's see what you got."

"We have yellow or white daisies. Two bits a bunch."

Millie signaled her approval, "Yes-yes-yes."

"We'll take them all," announced Duano.

Ida yelled again to the still-unseen Johnny. "Johnny, they want all the daisies!"

Looking to Duano, next she asked, "Do you already have your rings?"

Millie looked down at her own left hand. The White Owl Cigar band engagement ring was still there. Then she looked up to her intended husband and mouthed the word "ring."

He took the hint immediately. "Let's see what you've got in a plain band."

Ida nodded her understanding. She directed them to a small glass-topped display case in the back of the chapel.

Minister Johnny emerged from a curtain behind the raised altar. His long, horsey face was partially obscured by the daisies filling his hands and encircling arms. He stopped next to the altar, not wanting to interfere with the business his wife was conducting.

Ida pointed to each of the rings on display, announcing their prices. Plain gold or silver bands rested next to similar bands adorned with singleton faux diamonds. The couple both pointed to plain gold bands. From a shelf underneath the small display, a tray of gold bands, arranged by ring size, came out.

After fitting their rings, Ida directed the couple to the altar. She took the flowers from her husband as he straightened his narrow black tie and jacket lapels.

With a gold band in one hand, Millie accepted an armload of daisy bunches from Ida. "Please put the rest of the flowers in front of the altar but keep two bunches for you to hold."

Ida hugged Millie and whispered in her ear. "You look beautiful, darling, and I've never seen a more handsome groom."

Three minutes later Duano and Millie were married. Johnny Dodge, in practiced form, stepped down from the dais and shook their hands.

"Can I share the first toast with the newly married?" Not waiting for agreement, he retrieved a half-full bottle of Ezra Brooks bourbon and glasses from the lectern. After distributing the glasses, he poured one finger's depth of bourbon into each glass. Then came the toast, "To Mr. and Mrs...." and Ida in practiced fashion added "...Lagomarsino!"

The glasses now empty, Johnny directed Duano to follow him to the chapel office to conclude their business. As they walked, Johnny leaned in and whispered, "Do you need a room?"

* * * *

The newlyweds celebrated by having a quiet dinner at Luigi's restaurant. It overlooked the Coeur d' Alene Lake shore, just east of the city.

Duano chose a table in the corner of the dining room with a wall mural behind it. Venetian gondolas merged into Italian cypresses overlooking Lake Como. The new husband whispered to the waiter, "Could you bring a good bottle of wine to go with whatever the new Mrs. Lagomarsino orders?"

After a confirming nod the waiter left the two with menus. His next stop was a small table in the kitchen corner where a very large gentleman, wearing a dinner jacket over white shirt and tie, sat sipping a Campari cocktail. The boss had six identical sets of restaurant work clothes. His jacket, pants, and shirts were all necessarily custom made. When you're six foot nine inches tall, tip the scales at 320 pounds, and have an eighteen-inch neck, off-the-rack shopping is not an option.

"Boss, we've got newlyweds. Do you want me to comp them a dessert?"

The boss sipped his drink.

"Name?"

"Lagomarsino."

This roused the restauranteur into action. Luigi Brizzalera already knew that Primo's son was in Bayview. He also understood the value of having another 'family' member here with him in northern Idaho.

"Vince, these are my honored guests. Move them to the table in the corner by the window. Keep the tables around them clear. They are guests of the family: understood?"

"Yes, boss."

"Tell Frank to make a special dessert. Wines— Amarone for a red, Lacryma Christi for the white. I will go say hello. You get the new table ready."

Duano turned around when Millie lost her smile as the well-dressed giant approached the table. "I'm Luigi Brizzalerra, your host. You are Primo and Carmella's son?"

Duano acknowledged his family.

"Welcome and congratulations to you both."

Millie's smile returned as Duano introduced his bride.

"You are my honored guests tonight. I'd like you to have a special table." Brizz directed them across the dining room to be reseated next to the lake-view corner windows.

"When you've decided on your dinner, I'll have wine delivered to the table. Chef Frank is doing a special dessert for you."

Brizz pointed to the silent waiter, in jacket and tie, waiting off to the side. "Let Vince know whatever you need. I'll stop back after your dinner and maybe we can share a grappino." The giant turned and disappeared, leaving the table service to Vince.

* * * *

The two lovers shared one another in their marriage bed that night.

"Thank you for marrying me, babe. You could have done better if you really wanted, but you chose me. I love you so much."

"Ah, you're so sweet. I'm so happy. Come here, you big lug. I want to feel you close to me, tonight and every night. Thank you for keeping your promise to marry me. I love you, Duano."

"I love you too. I'll always keep my promises to you, babe. I'm sorry you don't have a diamond ring there instead of a plain gold band and the cigar band. Someday, I promise."

"I don't want diamonds, darling, just you and a family." Millie still had the secret of her past hidden. But neither Duano nor Millie knew about their share of life's little curve balls that fate had awaiting them.

8. Bayview 1947

Bonnie took the younger Millie under her wing and began making introductions to other Bayview wives. As their friendship grew, Bonnie became a mentor. Millie was eager to find a discreet teacher for the basic skills a young wife needs; cooking, sewing, and budgeting became tutorials. Her confidence grew incrementally as her domestic skills improved. Cooking experiments filled her free time while Duano was at work.

Bonnie and Royce were their first friends, but soon the social circle expanded to include Curtis and Betty. They had been at the station for three years. He ran the small print shop, and Betty was a secretary working in the Headquarters building. Inclusion in their neighbors' circle was much appreciated.

Pinochle or Hearts played at one of the three adjoining houses filled multiple nights per week. When the temperature was comfortable, the three couples began sharing potluck barbecues that rotated between their back yards.

It didn't take too many months for Royce and Curtis to become comfortable with the Lagomarsinos and reveal their darker sides. Over cards and burgers Duano learned Royce was some kind of minister or at least fancied himself as such. Royce had moved to North Idaho based on Curtis's report that the state was racially a monochromatic white.

In hindsight, the first clues had been Bible verse references shared between Royce and Curtis. Perhaps these were a test of Duano's racial sensitivity or biblical literacy? Millie's religious training was nonexistent. Duano's was Catholic in nature. It had ended when he acquired a taste for Lucky Strike cigarettes and enough savvy to contrive an absence from mass.

All subtlety had ended in the spring of 1947 when he joined the two neighbors for a round of target shooting.

"Duano, we're going to a piece of land I own. It's up on the rim rock above Hayden Lake," said Royce. The three of them got into his sedan, drove south on Highway 95 and turned east behind the lake.

Somewhere in a past geologic era a rift had been created on a straight north-south line several miles long. They headed south on the rim rock and stopped at a galvanized metal gate to the right of the roadway. Curtis opened the gate for Royce, who drove in and parked.

"These twenty acres are the future site of the compound of my 'Purity Church.' You and your wife are good, hard working whites. California and the whole West Coast have gone to hell. Between the blacks and the mud people bringing in crime, it's not where Curtis and I want our families. If you folks remember your Old Testament, the Aryans are God's chosen people. God commanded us not to marry outside our own race lest we corrupt our Aryan blood. We should be an Aryan Nation."

Royce waited for a response: agreement, disagreement or some sign that Duano was like-minded. When Duano didn't respond the reverend added the weight of his own brand of biblical justification.

"You don't have to believe me, son, believe your Bible. Go to Numbers 25 or Psalms 106. You'll see how Phineas saved the Israelites from plague by killing the race mixer. Read it for yourself."

"Who are the mud people?"

"Spiks, beaners, greasers; whatever you want to call them."

Then Curtis, who'd been a silent listener, spoke. "Now Royce, you know they don't like being called greasers. They insist on being called Lubracanos."

Royce smiled. "Then worst of all are the race traitors who marry outside our race, and the kikes." Royce added the last two groups on his 'hate list' with a firm nod. Curtis nodded in agreement and they both switched their eyes to Duano.

It hadn't been 30 years since Italians had been targets of "racial' discrimination. The targets had changed but not the hate.

"I thought we were going to put some holes in paper," Duano said, hoping to change the subject. The two nodded and smiled.

"Well let's get to it, then," said Royce, and pointed the way off to the right. Twenty yards ahead in a clearing was an improvised wood table and a bench for the shooter. Across the clearing sat an abandoned shed. Hay bales had been stacked against its side and old paper targets riddled with bullet holes hung from the bales. Curtis retrieved two Springfield rifles and a handful of targets from the trunk of the car. He handed a rifle to each of his companions, then removed the papers from under his arm.

"This is our 'running nigger' target. I print them up at work when nobody's looking." The crude image, black on white paper, was a cartooned profile. Kinky hair, big lips, wide open white eyes, an exaggerated butt and huge bare feet. Skinny arms bent at the elbows, pumping away with closed fists, completed the caricature.

"You got to shoot 'em on the run. Two in the body and when you get close enough, another one in the head.

That's what the Portuguese call the Mozambique method."

With three targets hung on the bale backstop against the shed, they took turns shooting from the bench rest. As Curtis took his turn, Royce narrated their vision for the future church compound.

"Just inside our front gate, there, will be the main building. The chapel, church office, and sanctuary are all going to be in one building. Across from the chapel will be a barracks for visiting pilgrims and other guests. Our rifle range will expand so we can train our young men for the coming conflict. This will all be inside our wire fence and a guard tower will be over by the new gate."

Duano said nothing as Royce shared his plan. "Curtis and I think that you and Millie would be comfortable as part of our group."

An answer was required to the implied invitation to join this little racist party. "I'll visit with my wife about this."

"Why?" asked Curtis, incredulous. "Women don't get a say. They do what their husbands decide."

"Curtis, you are not married to a redheaded farm girl. If she can castrate sheep, she can cut me. And I've got to sleep sometime. So, we'll talk." He now had a better appraisal of the two neighbors and no desire to be part of their Aryan Nation congregation.

That night Duano told Millie about his afternoon with Royce and Curtis.

"What you heard and saw sounds nasty. I don't hate anyone because of the color of their skin or their religion," said Millie. "If folks are nice to me, I am nice right back. I never knew any black folks and darn few Mexicans, but I don't hate any of them."

"I want nothing to do with their church. Royce and Bonnie, Curtis and Betty are all right as neighbors. Cards or a barbeque are fine, but for me it stops there. We'll be neighborly but I'm not interested in their church, agreed?"

And so it was agreed.

The Lagomarsinos maintained friendly social relations with both sets of neighbors. But neither Duano nor Millie got involved with the construction of Reverend Royce's church compound up on the Hayden Lake rim rock. In the months to come, Millie became Bonnie's helper at the Bayview store.

Duano had been a hunter for years in New Jersey. He became a hunting camp regular with Curtis. Curtis soon learned and thereafter respected Duano's aversion to any talk about religion at their nightly campfire. The two looked forward to their annual week together at Elk camp, a males-only get-away trip.

Money for the church's construction appeared to be a non-issue as the building and perimeter fence went up. By the spring of 1950 the church compound was complete. Royce and Curtis continued their employment at Bayview. Royce began to hold services at the compound in May 1950.

9. Frank, 1949

Frank Gagliardi and his brother, Vince, both enlisted in the Marines immediately after Pearl Harbor. Their motives were equal parts patriotism and desire to get away from an abusive mother. While they were in basic training at the Marine Recruit Depot, Parris Island, South Carolina, the call went out for volunteers for a new project.

In February 1942, Lieutenant Colonel Merritt Edson was looking for transfers to his revolutionary new unit. The 1st Marine Raider Battalion organized by "Red Mike" Edson was the prototype for every future Marine Raider Battalion formed during World War II. The Marine Raiders were to be "an elite force within an elite force." They were the first American unit ever allowed to use a human skull as the image on their unit shoulder patch.

Frank and Vince both volunteered. After their initial training and advanced work as scout-snipers, Vince was assigned to Company L, 3rd Marine Raider's Battalion commanded by Lt. Col. Harry Liversedge. Vince Gagliardi died on Bougainville.

Frank remained in the 1st Raider Battalion and was one of the defenders of Henderson Field on Guadalcanal. He fought in the Tarawa landing. Severely wounded during the fighting on Saipan, he spent 19 months in the Oak Knoll Navy hospital at Oakland, California, before being medically discharged in 1947.

After his discharge, Frank began stealing cars and robbing stores. Combat fatigue was as yet barely understood or appreciated by the authorities in their treatment of the 23-year-old criminal. Friends and relatives wondered why couldn't he just behave? The fact that he had been killing people while fighting for his own life since the age of 17 didn't factor into their thinking. He never talked about the dead Japanese who visited him nightly in his sleep.

But Frank's service record did occasionally help him in the courts. Prosecution was declined on many of his less serious crimes because of what he'd done during the war. Still, he was a convicted felon with prison sentences on his record. With only more prison or violent death looming in his future, his father reached out to the crime family that protected their neighborhood. "Please help our boy."

The family responded by sending Frank to Idaho. It was there Frank met Brizz, a World War I Marine 'Devil Dog' who'd survived the Belleau Woods fighting. Brizz had been an enforcer for the Lagomarsino family until the New Jersey climate became unhealthy for him to remain. Brizz introduced Frank to the peace of cooking. Frank was saved by the kitchen at "Luigi's by the Lake."

Still, Frank's dreams of Japanese dead persisted. He heard the sounds of infiltrators crawling through Marine lines on Guadalcanal, the glint of their knives covered by the soot that blackened the blades. The same Japanese women and even children, each with a grenade in hand, still walked towards him from the shadows like they had done on Saipan. He hid guns all around so one was always in reach for when the Japs came again. The medals that he'd won stayed hidden away in a box. Frank respected the medals but didn't want them in his life anymore.

10.   Stanley, 1950

Stanley Romano, the only child of an underboss, had been a brawler since grade school. Over the years, a wide arc of victims had forgiven much because of Stanley's father. But age had not improved his disposition or increased his tolerance or his respect for property and authority. At age 17 Stanley graduated from petty crime.

The mother of Stan's classmate called Stanley's aunt.

"Marjory, your little shit nephew is drunk again. He wants to fight everybody with a dick and screw everybody without one. He's ruining the kids' party. Can you please come get him? There's no one home at his parents'."

Shit! Again? was Marjorie's immediate t. "I'll come over now. I'm sorry. He's been a challenge for us all. You're a saint. Thanks for not calling the cops on the little asshole."

Marjory found Stanley, silent and sullen, sitting at the curb outside the party. Rolling down her car window, she yelled across the street to the budding hoodlum.

"Get in here. I'll take you home." With a scowl on his face, the teen rose from the curb and climbed into his aunt's car. She pulled away from the curb before asking.

"What did you do?"

"What did I do?" His voice raising now, Stanley slapped the metal dashboard with his palm. "What did I do? See, everybody always blames me," his tone switching to a whine of victimization.

"Listen, you are getting too old for this shit." Marjory's voice was also rising, matching the volume of her nephew. "You're eighteen in a few months and your father won't be able to clean up your messes. Get your head out of your ass!"

The heat of the car's cab, along with the internal heat of alcohol all contributed to the snap. Without another word spoken, Stanley slid a switch-blade knife from his front pocket and popped open the blade. He leaned over towards his aunt as she drove and placed the blade against her neck. His eyes were dilated, and his nostrils flared as he stared into her face. She could apologize or even confirm his victimhood, he t. But that was not what he got.

Her eyes drifting from the road to Stanley and back, as she pulled the car to the curb.

"You don't have the balls!"

A jolt of testosterone flared like gasoline squirted onto a fire. But he did have "the balls." In those last moments, an arterial spray coated the wheel and windshield and silenced Marjory's voice forever.

* * * *

Uncle Primo's last gift to Stanley's father was to spare the life of his son. Stanley was given a banishment of indeterminate length to Idaho. Primo's man in north Idaho, Luigi Brizzalera, took 17-year-old Stanley into his home. He was too young and too unpredictable to be left on his own. Brizz became a constant in Stanley's life and by his mere presence exerted needed control over the killer teen.

"Kid, you are here with me as your last chance." They sat across a steel-topped prep table in the giant's restaurant kitchen.

"Your Uncle let you live on three conditions. You never show your face on the east coast. You never mention your connection to the family and you never embarrass the family. Your life and my life are now tied together. If you shame the family again, I'm responsible. Your life is in my hands, because my life is in Primo's." Brizz and Stanley sat silently at the table, the teen unsure what was expected.

"Do you understand the rules?" Brizz asked. Stanley nodded but remained silent and so did Brizz, setting the pattern that instructions were given only once.

Childhood was officially ending there and then. Stanley would be treated like a man or erased as a potential threat to the family. The implication of Primo's message, delivered by Brizz, had to be enough. Cajoling or threatening was not the family's way. Stanley was confronted with the hard facts of his new life.

"You are now a junior dishwasher in my restaurant. I want you to meet your boss. Frank, come over here for a minute."

Frank Gagliardi put down the long-bladed knife he was using to slice eggplant for tonight's Eggplant Parmesan. He wiped his hands on a kitchen towel as he stood silently across from his boss. Frank already knew the young man's backstory and the rules by which he'd live or die.

"Stanley, meet Frank. Now look outside, kid. See all those trees?"

The young killer nodded.

"Frank, here, has killed more Japs than the number of all those trees." He turned to Frank.

"Stanley is a second dishwasher for your kitchen. He will stay in the downstairs room at my place. For now, he's either at my place or here. Understood?" The silent chef nodded his understanding as Brizz stood up.

"Grab your suitcase from my car and I'll show you where you stay. My wife, Sophia—Mrs. Brizzalera to you—will cook those meals that you don't get in the restaurant kitchen. My home is behind the restaurant. In 30 minutes, be back here ready to work. Frank will see you're fed and tell you how to do your job."

11. Eleanor

Eleanor Greenberg was 12 when her family arrived at Auschwitz-Birkenau in 1943. She was separated from her parents, Rachael and Shlomo, and her brother Efrym. Like her brother, she received a camp ID: six numbers tattooed on the inside of her left forearm. Her parents and brother did not escape the gas chamber and crematorium.

Eleanor was saved by her flawless white complexion, perfect features and immature body. Herr Doktor Werner Kleinheintz had selected her as his new indulgence. The doctor was not unique among pedophiles in that he had a strong preference for pre-pubic females of a specific age. No boys, no children and no body hair or breasts.

Eleanor was perfect. She was saved by genetics that had granted her a late onset to puberty. She got to live, even if rape and forced sodomy were the alternatives to death in the gas chamber. Eleanor learned to hide away her hate for Werner. She never forgot the metal banner above the rail tracks at the main gate of Auschwitz. "Arbeit Macht Frei—Work sets you free." She'd survive at all cost. Her human spirit could be dampened by circumstance but never extinguished.

She attended to her duties with the same dedication of any other slave who wanted to live more than die. As her budding breasts began to betray her, fate intervened. Auschwitz was abandoned by the Nazis just before the Red Army arrived in January 1945.

On Werner's final morning at the camp, he gifted her with life. The Doktor had fallen in love with the young Jewess. "I'll come for you after the war, my love," were his parting words as he hid her in a closet. Her reply, spoken with equal sincerity, "Don't worry Werner, I'll find you, now save yourself—for me." Eleanor Greenberg meant every word she'd said.

* * * *

Eleanor fled west from Auschwitz. She feared the Russians as much as she hated the Nazis. Reaching the Allied Army lines in Germany brought her to safety in a displaced persons camp where she turned 16. A secret British army unit of Jewish volunteers worked to organize the exodus of 250,000 Jewish refugees to Palestine, in defiance of the British authorities. Most of their refugee ships were turned back, but not all.

Eleanor turned 17 in a Kibbutz overlooking the Sea of Galilee. There she met Malachi Wald. Wald and four other former partisans formed a secret assassins' network; DAHLED, YOD, NUN—"The blood of Israel will take vengeance." They abbreviated the full name to: DIN, which is the Hebrew word for "judgement." Eleanor, young, fit and harboring a special hate for the Nazis, became one of their assassins.

Former partisan fighters taught her the finer points of following a trail and getting close to her target. Eleanor learned the dark arts of close-quarters combat with hands, knives or improvised weapons.

"Remember Eleanor, the blade always faces out. You don't stab, you filet. A strike to the throat will silence your prey." Lev, a butcher before the war, explained how to relieve the gasses produced during putrification of a body. He showed where to cut to prevent submerged corpses from floating back to the surface.

Besides the weapons, she learned to barter for information once she'd secured her target. Her question was, "Who else do you know? If you can give me a bigger fish, I'll throw you back." Often these disarmed cowards, believing her lie, offered up bigger fish. But it didn't matter; they all died after her final words, "Look who's killing you: a Jew."

12. Doktor Werner Kleinheintz

By 1946 Werner Kleinheintz was working for the US Navy at Bayview, Idaho. Both the US and Russia, competitors now, saw value in the research of defeated enemies like Werner and his counterparts in the V-2 rocket and jet engine programs, Each side absorbed as many scientists as they could get their hands on. The doctor had led the Reich's efforts to perfect cold weather, waterproof clothing for their navy. He tried survival suit linings of felted hair from dead Jews. Next were oiled silk survival suits padded and lined with Jewish skin still insulated by a layer of cured body fat. Both failed. Werner pressed on, with no shortage of test subjects who died in the cold with each failed test.

Werner had come to Auschwitz from the German Navy's research station on the shores of Lake Toplitz. He was also an expert on how cold affected the sonic signature of metal. His work for the German Navy would have gone into the next generation of U boats. The Type XXI's would have soon appeared, had not the exigencies of war prevented it.

Lake Toplitz is in the high mountains between Bavaria and Austria. Werner found Bayview to be similar. He'd been invited to Bayview in 1946 to continue his research about temperature and sonic signatures. This esoteric field was a hot topic for submarine designers.

He had avoided being tried for war crimes by the thinnest of reasons. The testing on humans had been done by others—the bad Nazis. He'd convinced his interrogators that he had always and only been a man of science, never politics. He was a good German: a scientist with future value for the Allies. True, he had been a party member, as membership was required to work for the

Reich. They could not prove he had been a good Nazi. Thus his sins were all forgiven, or at least forgotten.

With the war lost, Nazi leadership created an underground army of young men who had grown up during the Reich years. They called themselves *"die Werwolfs."* They were expected to keep the Nazi ideology alive until the Reich could rise again. Richard Baer, the last commandant of Auschwitz, had appointed Werner to guide one group of *Werwolfs*.

* * * *

While working at Bayview, he listened for and found Nazi sympathizers. Their veiled racism was not that far from the overt race hate of the Reich. Werner met Royce and Curtis, who also worked at Bayview. Over time, their proximity at work brought them together at the same lunch table in the little town of Bayview. Their shared beliefs were soon unmasked, each to the other.

Royce and Curtis shared their plans for a 'whites only' homeland in the Pacific Northwest. Beyond dreams, the two shared with Werner their methods. Royce's planned 'Purity Church' would proffer biblical references showing the penalty for race mixing was death.

Royce and Curtis hated Jews. Werner saw Jews as convenient targets and slaves. *After all, if we killed all the Jews, we'd only have to find someone else to blame.*

Werner kept a low profile in his dealings with Reverend Royce. With his ties to the *Werwolfs*, he saw opportunities in the race-hating reverend to advance his cause by identifying local white supremacists. Over the ensuing months he carefully brokered a deal; Nazi gold for future accommodations of *Werwolfs* in north Idaho.

Money began flowing in 1949. It came routed through ex-Nazi contacts in Chile to other 'good Germans' now living in the United States. Former Auschwitz guards Hubert Schwarz and Hans Schnabel, whose Nazi crimes had gone undiscovered, delivered the cash.

In the fall of 1950, the two former guards moved to the Hayden Lake church compound. Both earned their keep by working as guard-caretakers and by improving the rifle range to better train future Aryan youth.

Werner had a second mission for the Reich. He would help with its return by spying on American submarine technological developments at Bayview. He dreamed of being hailed as a hero of the Fourth Reich. They would remember him as helping birth the Reich in a new 'whites only' homeland. He'd also be the man of science who helped the Reich's future navy build the greatest, most lethal submarine fleet that had ever sailed. What magnificent legacies!

13.   Rudolpho, aka Randall, 1951

Primo Lagomarsino called his son, Duano. The family was sending a cousin, Rudolpho Antonini, out to cool off. Randall Albers was his working name. A dishonorably discharged navy seaman, he had remade himself into a naval Commander. He knew the uniforms, the language and the places to look for his chosen prey. He'd had a good run as Randall Albers until now. Randall simply picked the wrong victim in wife number five.

* * * *

Randall arrived by train in Spokane, Washington in the summer of 1951. There to meet him were the giant, Brizz, and Duano. With Randall's few suitcases loaded in Duano's Ford, the three headed back east and then turned north on Highway 41 to Spirit Lake, Idaho. West along the south lakeshore they drove, stopping at the arch-topped drive that disappeared off into the trees. Hung above the arch was a simple sign, 'Shady Rest Resort.'

The single blacktop lane wound through a hundred yards of mature conifers to the lakeshore. The lane fronted a chain of cabins, each with its own parking spot. Opposite the cabins across the lane were three buildings. First in line was the smallest of the three. The sign above the door read 'Laundry.' Next was the combination restroom and shower building. Farther along the lane was the camp office and grocery store. Brizz motioned for Duano to pull over at the last cabin in the lakeside row.

"Randall, welcome to your new home. You have credit inside the store, and your charges come to me. Wait here with Duano while I get the key," and the giant strode off toward the office.

"So, how long am I stuck here?"

"You're here until my father thinks it's safe for you to leave."

"This is a bunch of shit. I was doing fine. I move on and I'm good"

Duano regarded this piece of wasted humanity. *I never thought my dad hated me. Why did he stick me with such an asshole? The world would be a better place without this guy.* "Yeah, life's a bitch."

Key now in hand, Brizz returned. Crossing the small covered porch, he opened the cabin door. Randall stepped into the doorway and stared into the gloom. An iron-framed double bed was next to a three-drawer chest along the wall. Two well-used club chairs separated by a scuffed wooden table and a single floor lamp completed the furnishings.

"This is your home until New Jersey decides otherwise."

"Do I get a car?" asked Randall.

"No, but you get to live as long as you keep your mouth shut." Brizz punctuated the direction by giving a painful squeeze to the new arrival's shoulder. "If you do what you're told, I'll bring a girl by every couple of weeks."

"That's all I get?"

Brizz reached out to the corner of the porch and retrieved a single rod and reel.

"Learn to fish. Read a book, for Christ's sake," and with that he and Duano left.

* * * *

Randall specialized in middle-aged women of questionable beauty. Some were recent widows, others, divorcees. Some were wannabes who'd never been invited to the big marital dance. His hunting grounds were the upscale cocktail lounges outside different navy bases. He had plied the entire East Coast from Florida up through Virginia and finally to Brooklyn.

His con was refined and well rehearsed. A four-week program with five simple, heartless steps: find 'em— bed 'em —wed 'em —dupe 'em —dump 'em.

The con was also low risk. Illegal wearing of a military uniform is only a misdemeanor. A small fine or a brief probation were the only likely consequences.

Randall also didn't see a bigamy charge as a big risk. Any middle-aged woman in a bar at mid-day was easy pickings. They wanted what he was peddling. These women desperately wanted to hold more than the cocktails in their hands. They never wanted to believe they'd been conned. He left each victim with a plausible belief that someday he'd be back. The victims supplied the other necessary element: not wanting to admit to themselves they were alone again. He made himself appear to be the proverbial 'last popsicle in hell.'

Week One: Any cocktail lounge located near a navy base was fine. He sat two stools away: not too intrusive, not too distant. He used a subtle approach, never staring: glances, smiles, nods, and an offered drink. Trim and well groomed, in a naval commander's uniform, the polite stranger acted admiring and then attentive.

"I apologize for staring. I'm just back in the country and on shore for the first time since the Korean war started. You can't imagine how refreshing it is to see a beautiful, mature white woman. I hope my boldness doesn't offend you." This he'd say with a self-effacing sag of his shoulders.

"May I buy you a drink? My name is Randy and you might have guessed from the uniform, I'm in the Navy. I'm a flyer," and he'd point to the silver wings on his chest.

The plan might unfold in several different ways. It might be drinks, then dinner or better yet, petting with an intoxicated woman in the front seat of her car. Maybe he even got invited home to her bed. When in doubt, he had a clincher.

"Well, it's been great, but I better get back aboard, if I don't want to be sleeping on the sidewalk. The shore patrol frowns on that." If that pure gold line didn't get him between her sheets, he'd move on.

Week Two: They'd screw until they were both dizzy. He'd spend his seed money on flowers, a rental car for himself, dinners out and lots of drinks. He'd be every middle-aged single woman's dream, as innocent and smooth as Baby Jesus in velvet pants.

Week Three: Set the hook. "My month of shore leave is half gone. Now this may sound crazy, but I've never met a girl like you before. I'm having the time of my life. You don't mind my quirks. My getting up at 5 A.M. or my disappearing for morning runs. Anyway," pause and then with trepidation in his voice ask, "Would you marry me?"

If the answer was 'No', he moved on to another target. If yes, then he'd move to 'Phase four' after all the wedded bliss she could handle, and he could stand. The morning runs provided convenient access to Randall's partners of choice: other men.

Week Four: "We better get our financial houses in order before I'm back to sea. I can get only one weekly morale radio-telephone call. I'll go to the base today with a copy of our marriage license and get you made the beneficiary for my insurance. I'll also put your name on my credit union account. Tomorrow we should go to your bank and get me on your checking and saving accounts."

With his access to her money established, it was time to prepare his exit. It went something like this: Pick a quiet moment. At her breakfast table always worked.

"You have a right to know something I couldn't tell you before. I shouldn't even tell you now. But you are my wife," he'd say with emphasis.

"I fly for a joint Navy-CIA operations group in Southeast Asia. There will be times when," strategic pause, "I won't be able to communicate with you. I may be gone for long periods," pause again. "My time is controlled by the mission, however long it takes. I do what the country needs me to be doing." Another pause and taking her hand, he delivered the clincher.

"I just don't want you to worry. I will be back." Wait for her hug-tears-or-whatever to subside. Then in passing mention, "I might draw from our accounts while I'm overseas. This is 'flash money,' to help me play a part or cover unforeseen expenses. So, don't worry if you see an unexpected withdrawal."

The Exit: "I can't face seeing you on the dock when my ship pulls out. I'd rather say our goodbyes here and now, from our bed. I want my last image to be of you, naked with a big smile on your face. Would you do that for me?"

They always said, "Yes."

By now her cash flow was studied. How he'd milk this cow was now planned. He'd use reassuring letters about his Navy pay being deposited in their credit union account. It's just not accessible to either of them from his ship. Could he get more out of her over a period of months or in a simple one-time draining of all their accounts?

* * * *

Bernadette Albers, wife number five, had not gone quietly as had her predecessors. Her money and hope were both exhausted six months after Randall's final goodbye. In the spring of 1951, she went to the Public Information Officer at the New London, Connecticut base. Hoping her beloved was out doing secret things, she found instead that no such person as Randall Albers was even in the Navy. Bernie's anger fueled her already vindictive nature.

Bernie 'the Bag,' as she was known, was the sister of Wade 'the Blade' Bagdaserian, an Armenian-American crime boss from Philadelphia. Wade's delight at his sister's long-awaited nuptials changed to a white-hot rage and promise of bloody revenge after Randall fled. An investigation had begun concerning Randall's disappearance.

Next she went to the local FBI office. They took her information, offered sympathy and promptly shit-canned the report when she left.

She located New London's own staff writer for the Navy Times. The bi-weekly paper was available free to all active duty and retired Navy personnel and their dependents. Bernie hoped that a Navy Times story about Randall Albers would lead her to other women who had also been victims.

Sure enough, within three months Bernie was sharing her story with Alfie, wife # 1 from Gulfport, Mississippi. Helen, the second Mrs. Albers, was from Pensacola. Hazel from Newport News placed third, and Flora from Portsmouth, Maine had just preceded Bernie. They all told the same story of seduction and theft. Or as Hazel put it, "screwed twice, only kissed once." The five agreed to meet in a location central to them all: Charlotte, North Carolina.

At the meeting they agreed to hunt down their swine of a husband and take back whatever cash they could. After that, they would wreak a bitter revenge. Alfie, who'd Americanized her name from that of her Afghani mother, 'Alfsoon,' suggested the traditional Afghani woman's treatment for rapists.

Randall's fate was now chosen. Bernie agreed to use her brother's contacts to find a skilled people hunter and executioner. She told Wade what they wanted.

* * * *

Wade 'the Blade' found Eleanor through his underworld connections. The Armenian diaspora had scattered his forebears all over the Middle East, including Israel.

Eleanor had left the DIN after several years. Her singular talents kept her in demand within the criminal world. Lots of well-connected people knew and used Eleanor for their own sensitive wet work.

In the criminal world, every piece of information has its price. It wasn't hard to find someone in the Mob who, for the right price, pointed Eleanor to a small town in North Idaho, Spirit Lake, and the 'Shady Rest Resort.'

Wade 'the Blade' also provided Eleanor with Bernie the Bag's phone number and a picture of Randall bedecked in his Naval Commander's uniform. Eleanor flew from the East Coast to Spokane, Washington, where she rented a car and studied maps for a full day.

Next, she assembled her toolkit for kidnapping and murder. Each item was purchased at a different local hardware store, so she made no memorable purchases. Duct tape, a knife, heavy cord, an improvised leather sap, and cloth for a blindfold completed her kit.

Last on her list was camouflage suitable for this one particular job. At a rural mountain lake resort, Eleanor would fit into the background in fisherman's gear. A floppy hat obscured her face, and a fisherman's vest hid her size and build. With a fishing pole in hand, she became just another anonymous stranger.

Once she was equipped, a day trip to find the 'Shady Rest Resort' took her 30 miles east and into Idaho for the first time. A well-marked two-lane highway ran north through Idaho to the Canadian border, passing through Spirit Lake. Eleanor didn't leave the highway, but pulled into the graveled lot of the Busy Bee café.

While waiting for her order to arrive, she studied an illustrated map of the area and picked up a Chamber of Commerce brochure. This was all she needed for now. A sandwich and Coke later, she continued driving north. At the edge of town, she turned off the highway and followed a residential street to the lakeshore. Driving along the pine-lined road, she kept a watchful eye for the resort. She passed the arched portal complete with a 'Shady Rest Resort' sign. Eleanor maintained her leisurely pace, stopping a quarter mile farther on in a shady roadside rest overlooking the lake.

She took her gear from the trunk of the car, suited up and walked through the line of trees to the lakeshore. There she set off fishing her way back towards the resort. Every hundred feet she stopped to make several casts with her spinning rod into the green water before moving on. When the line of cabins and resort buildings came in sight, Eleanor stayed in character. She moved along the shore a few yards at a time, stealing glances into the camp as she went.

She knew Randall's face and build. There he was, sitting in a folding chair beside the first cabin to come into view. As she kept her watch, their eyes met, so she raised a hand in recognition as any friendly fisherman might. Randall responded by waving back with his middle finger and going into the cabin.

Hmm, so that's how the city boy enjoys being parked in the woods. Keeping in character, she fished on until the resort was out of sight along the lakeshore. There she cut through the woods to the road and back to her rental car.

In her room that night, the day's experiences furthered Eleanor's developing plan. When she revisited the Chamber of Commerce brochure, her attention lit on an oddity of the lake.

Spirit Lake had a sealed bottom because of a layer of Precambrian era clay. But near the lumber mill site, naturally occurring sink holes came and went. The sinks, when located, were filled with gravel and resealed with bags of Wyoming Bentonite clay powder. Each hole drained large amounts of water and sucked down anything on the bottom, which was lost forever. How could she make use of the new information? Ah yes! This area, called the 'mill pond,' was a natural site for a body dump. Eleanor's plan gelled.

The illustrated brochure from the café showed the mill's location and mill pond site on the lake. Bordering the illustrated map were ads for local businesses: fishing guides, resorts, motels, bars and restaurants. She would check out the two resorts closest to the mill pond. Did they have separate cabins and boats for guests? First, came inquiring phone calls, and then a site visit.

Eleanor found the situation she wanted at the 'Edgewater Resort', which was directly across the mill pond from the 'Shady Rest.' Their cabins were separated by lawn and a good gravel road that connected each inside its forested setting. Each cabin also included its own 12 ft. aluminum boat. The setting was as promised, 'A quiet getaway site for relaxation or fishing.' Everything was subject to Bernie's approval. That night she outlined the plan in a call to Bernie.

Randall the asshole, who had flipped her off, would arrive bound and gagged in her aluminum boat and be kept in her cabin. The wives would have cabins at the resort for a sorority reunion weekend. Randall's punishment would take place at her cabin just before the wives departed. She'd take his remains by boat out to the middle of the mill pond and dump him. Her own departure would follow leisurely the next day. This was one weekend of revenge for the five wives and $5,000 for her.

Bernie the Bag liked the plan and after consulting with the other wives agreed to set a date for the weekend. 'The Bag' called back two days later and their date was set. She'd send Eleanor half of her fee plus deposit money for three cabins. Eleanor would send back reservations under five fake names, travel directions and a timetable. The event would take place in two weeks.

* * * *

The snatch of the sleeping Randall from his cabin, two weeks later, went perfectly. First two knocks on the door, then two quick knocks on his head and he was ready for his first boat ride. Eleanor dragged the unconscious figure to her aluminum boat and rowed across the lake to her cabin at the Edgewater Resort. Bound and gagged, Randall spent the night on Eleanor's cabin floor.

An audible slap awakened Randall. Bernie the Bag's face filled his field of vision.

"Randall, have you ever heard the old saying that payback is a bitch?" When no response came, she grabbed his jaw, squeezing his cheeks hard, her face lowered to just above his nose. Her breath was hot as she shook his head from side to side and repeated, "Have you heard that?"

Through pain and pucker his attempt at "yes" came just above a whisper.

"Well I'm the bitch. By the way, you would have been shocked at the mob's low estimation of your value. Protecting a shirttail relative from a pissed-off ex-wife is not a priority."

Bernie motioned to Eleanor, who was kneeling by her side, that she was done for the moment. She moved over to the bed, joining her sister-wives.

Five Mrs. Randalls watched in a semi-circle of hate-filled victims. They had all lost their money and some of them their homes to Randall's four-week program. Most had also sacrificed their intangibles; self-image, self-respect and worst of all, the ability to trust any man.

The five sat side by side on the bed in the resort cabin. With them were the means to their desired end. Alfie, wife number one, quietly smiled with foreknowledge of what was to come. Helen, the second Mrs. Randall, was in an animated conversation with Flora, wife number four. Hazel, who'd been third in the marital scam, looked worried, and Bernie, as per usual, looked angry.

"Are you sure no one will find out what we're doing?" asked Hazel. Her question was directed to no one in particular as she tried to sit still and control her constant furtive glances and hand wringing.

Alfie and Bernie eyed one and other. Alfie scooted closer to Hazel and took her hands in her own.

Bernie beamed a reassuring smile at the group's weak sister. "No worries. Eleanor is the best, and we'll be gone in a couple hours. Nobody is going to find his body, so they won't even know he's dead for days. That is, if anybody gives a shit."

Before them, Randall Albers lay bound and gagged on a large blanket-covered rubber sheet. The wives opened the first cans from a case of Pabst beer Bernie had furnished. Alfie, as a Moslem, chose tea for her beverage. She also brought the one special tool for their revenge. As they drank, all watched Randall squirm. Each shared her own story of loss. The home, the plans, the dreams each had lost, they now recounted to their husband.

Waiting until all twenty-four beers were drunk, Eleanor finally asked, "Are you ladies ready?" A chorus of four hissed "Yesses" signaled it was time. Hazel waited her turn in pale silence.

"Alfie you're up," said Eleanor as she knelt and placed gloved hands on either side of Randall's head.

She removed the gag from his mouth as Alfie joined her on the floor, the small wreath in hand. Randall's eyes widened at the sight of the wreath of Hawthorne thorns. Eleanor silenced the cries by gripping his nose between her thumb and forefinger. Alfie stuck the wreath into Randall's mouth, smiling as she did. His head tried to thrash from side to side but Eleanor's hands kept his mouth facing up. The wreath of thorns kept his mouth open.

95

Each wife knew what was coming next and had prepared herself with drink. At the first kick of his legs, the waiting four sat down, two women on each leg. Each ex-wife took her turn, squatting over his mouth and emptying her bladder. Randall drowned in their urine sometime between the final two contributors.

Helen and Flora, true to old habits learned in a high school lavatory, high-fived one another. Hazel, the third contributor, watched Flora and Bernie who followed her over Randall. Hazel's pallor faded to white. She covered her mouth and ran to the bathroom, holding her acid spew of beer and breakfast until she reached the toilet.

Bernie and Alfie shared satisfied smiles. "I'll stay in touch with all of you" said Bernie to the group. As each Mrs. Randall left, Bernie shared a final hug. With her departing hug, Alfie whispered, "Keep an eye on Hazel. She's fragile."

"Yes."

Bernie turned to Eleanor and counted 25 hundred-dollar bills. For Eleanor, Randall had been strictly business. Not so for Bernie.

"You look sad. What are you feeling right now?" asked Eleanor.

"I thought I'd feel happy or maybe relieved when he was gone, but I don't. I'm angry."

"Angry at Randall?"

"No, angry at myself." Bernie sat back down on the bed and nudged her husband's corpse with the toe of her shoe.

"I've got a body like a fireplug. I'm as soft as a bag of hammers and swear like a longshoreman. I'm mad at myself for being so stupid, so desperate that I fell for him." The seated Bernie began to sob softly as Eleanor joined her on the bed.

"Look, it's none of my business. You thought you needed him, so you were willing to believe the louse. Now you know that you didn't need him. No man is going to fool you again."

Together they sat for a full five minutes until Bernie's wave of emotion passed. Eleanor helped Bernie outside to her car and watched silently as she drove away

Eleanor remained behind after the women left and began her work disposing of Randall's body. First, she cut away his clothing, not worrying about accidental nicks since Randall was way beyond caring or even bleeding. Then she made careful cuts to the corpse, preventing it from floating when gasses inevitably developed. The body dump, performed that same night, went off unnoticed as the corpse quietly slipped below the moon-lit surface of Spirit Lake.

After opening all her cabin windows to disperse the odor of urine, Eleanor folded the blanket inside the rubber sheet. The parcel was then taped shut with duct tape. Odorless now, the two ground cloths would depart with her tomorrow when she turned in the group's room keys. Driving out of the resort and back through town, she stopped at the Busy Bee Café for a celebratory breakfast. Another job well done.

Over her second of cup of coffee and the final bites of hash browns, Eleanor found herself at ease in the north Idaho environment. Compared to her previous urban homes, this place was quiet. The air was clean and the dappled sun through the trees was inviting rather than fearful like city shadows. She thought about the Kibbutz and the winds that blew across the Sea of Galilee. *I think I'd like it here.*

She remembered that the DIN network had tracked Doktor Kleinheintz to the United States, but specifically where had not yet been determined. They knew that Werner had become an Allied war prize. Eleanor's patient hunt for this particular monster had never ended and never would until one of them was dead.

Instead of going directly back to Spokane, Eleanor retrieved a map from her rental car. She plotted out a quick driving tour of the area. She'd continue north to visit all the small towns as far north as Sandpoint. Her route would then return south through Sagle, Athol, Bayview, and Hayden Lake before turning west at Coeur d' Alene.

She preferred to be near a major highway rather than on one. The scenery and the low price for housing delighted her, but by far, she liked little Bayview best.

Lake Pend Oreille was gorgeous. The air was crisp and smelled of pine. National forest land surrounded the town on three sides with the lakeshore on the other; all could be escape routes if ever necessary. Bayview was smaller than many of her other options, but the essentials — stores, post office and bar — were all there. Only three miles off the main highway and 40 miles to an airport, it would be a good place to keep her life separate from her work. Examining the Bayview option filled her mind on the flight back east.

What passed for home in New York was a rented one-bedroom apartment deliberately unadorned by personal touches. Eleanor had lived out of her suitcase much of the last 18 months since she'd left Israel. A hunt had taken her to New York City. Now a hunt had introduced her to Bayview, Idaho and just perhaps a new home somewhere her professional and personal lives could finally coexist, separate but equal.

A planner by nature, Eleanor set about the task of relocation. She let her bosses know that she would be unavailable to them for the next month. Next she prepaid a month's rent, so her New York life stayed in play, just suspended for now. Her bank account held over $20,000, not counting the final Spirit Lake payment. She informed her banker that a change of scene might be coming up. The banker arranged a point of contact for a funds transfer to a cooperating Spokane bank.

When she flew out again from New York, Eleanor took the same route back to Spokane, rented a car and found lodging in Coeur d' Alene, Idaho. Next came a day trip to Bayview to check out the town more closely. When nothing she found discouraged her, she stopped in at the town's only real estate office to ask about rentals. Any thought of buying was still premature. She'd live here as a renter first to see if the town suited her. Choices for immediate occupancy were limited. She settled on a vacation cabin at the edge of the national forest northeast of town. With her deposit paid, keys in hand and cabin inspected, she returned to Coeur d'Alene. She moved to Bayview the next day.

Over the weeks, Bayview proved a good choice. Eleanor settled the final details of her move. Using a rental car was out, so she purchased a used DeSoto sedan. Her remaining clothes and few possessions arrived from New York. She rented a post office box in the name on her New York license, Ellen Ripley, age 22.

The real Ellen Ripley died as an infant. The all-important date of birth and names of parents were chiseled on the infant's gravestone. With this information, Eleanor had applied for a duplicate birth certificate. Then using this document as identification, a New York driver's license with Eleanor's picture soon followed. library card, Macy's card and local apartment rental agreement completed the fabrication of the Ellen Ripley persona. The word went out to the mob. She was back in play.

Eleanor Greenberg, the killer from New York, had become Ellen Ripley, a trust fund baby who played at being a travel writer. This back-story eliminated questions about the source of her income. Any travel was just part of her job. Ellen also made her more of a gentile. Al she had been a non-religious Jew, being a non-religious gentile was a better fit in north Idaho.

* * * *

The following month, Bernie kept her promise to Hazel. "I'm checking like I said I would. How are you doing? You were pretty upset by Spirit Lake, I know. I was upset too, so I wanted to see how you were getting along?"

There was only silence on the other end of the line.

"I guess I wanted the revenge more before we got it than I enjoyed it after. It just made me sad because I finally realized how I'd let myself turn into a victim. Anyway, I thought you were a really nice person and more sensitive than me. Growing up with a brother who told me that my face looked like a 'slapped ass,' made me kind of insensitive, I guess. Anyway, I'd like to stay in touch, if that's all right with you?"

Long moments of silence on the line followed. Bernie heard Hazel softly sobbing.

"I'll call again next week. Hang in there, kiddo. We're both fine."

14.   Bayview, Early 1952

The dry goods and grocery store in the center of town adjoined the small city park. The park's neatly trimmed lawn sloped down from a flagpole flying the Stars and Stripes. Ellen decided to skip for now the diner, combination gas station-garage, 'Angler's Bait Shop' and the 'No Reservations Tavern.' Groceries came first, and if available, a decent vodka.

Millie answered the tinkle of the bell when Ellen entered. "Hello," she called from where she had been stacking cans for a display in the grocery half of the store. She had welcomed the opportunity for a part-time job and had been employed since late 1946, soon after they arrived in Bayview. Her friend, Bonnie, still managed the store but did backroom paperwork while Millie worked the front.

Pregnant for the second time and starting to show, Millie hoped for a better outcome than the 12-week miscarriage she'd suffered with her first pregnancy. True or not, she believed she was being denied a child, and blamed it on her days at Miss Della's brothel.

"Hello," Ellen answered back.

"I'm Millie. What can I do for you today?"

"I'm Ellen Ripley, but people call me 'El'," and she offered her hand.

Millie was uncertain if the rich college girl wanted to have her hand shaken or kissed. She shook.

"I just rented a cabin out that way." El pointed up the street towards the end of the road. "I'm just looking for a little peace and quiet. But I need to lay in some groceries and a bottle of vodka for a 5:00 P.M. vodka Collins on my porch."

"Well you came to the right place, but we can't sell anything stronger than 3% beer or table wine. 'No Reservations'," Millie pointed across the street. "They have a state liquor concession so they can sell you a bottle of vodka."

"I'm feeling better already, thanks! I see the groceries over on that side, so I'll go shop. Then home to see if there really is a decent writer trapped somewhere inside me." She took a chromed grocery cart from beside the cash register and started shopping. They chatted as Ellen shopped, and Millie returned to stocking shelves.

"So, what do you write?"

"I'm working on being a travel writer. My parents are both gone now. They left me some money when they passed. I was tired of being a college girl, so here I am. As long as the money lasts, I'm going to see what's out there beyond the borders of Maine where I grew up. I just need to write something and sell it."

"So how did you come to be in our little town?"

"In our library back in Bar Harbor, Maine, I found a book from the Union Pacific Railroad, and it had wonderful pictures of their trains and resorts. They own the Sun Valley ski resort here in Idaho. Anyway, their tracks go through these parts, and the pictures in the book were really attractive. So, here I am."

"Well if you do your shopping here in Bayview, I'll be seeing a lot of you. If you need anything else, directions or information, come on by. I'd be glad to help you with whatever you need."

Had the two women be able to hear each other's ts, they might have been surprised at the unintended start of their connection. *Well, she seems friendly enough. I wouldn't mind seeing her around.*

15. Ed, April 1952

Ed Verna had been driving truck for 15 years. For his efforts he had hemorrhoids, an extra hundred pounds of body fat and a three-pack a day cigarette habit. He'd left an anonymous trail of female victims whom he'd assaulted all over the west.

His most unforgettable experience was with a young blonde whore in a northern California whorehouse. Ed shuddered at the memory of how the straight razor gleamed in the dim red light of her room. He could still feel the razor's cold steel against his erection.

Ed made deliveries to military facilities. He'd never been to the Navy Research Station at Bayview before he rolled in on a cold April morning. *Ah shit, another stop out in East Jesus, Idaho or some other backwoods full of rubes and mental defectives.* The only good news was the nearby Indian reservation. Female Indian hitch hikers were easy victims. For a ride, a meal and a cheap bottle they seemed to go along with his program just fine.

Two of Duano's crew off-loaded his semi-truck, checked the goods against the shipping manifest and sent him on his way. Pulling out of the gate at Bayview, Ed saw both the tavern and the diner at the same time. First food and then beer were his priorities. "Why not!" he said aloud, inside his empty truck cab. The length of his vehicle ruled out the diner's parking lot, so he pulled to a stop along a row of houses across from the diner.

As he climbed down from the truck a very pregnant woman came out of one house and crossed the street ahead of him, walking towards the store. They passed quickly and quietly as strangers. Ed sat next to the diner's front window, eating greasy enchiladas and longing for a beer to wash them down. He could see the same pregnant woman at the store next door. She'd come outside to sweep the narrow sidewalk between store and street.

The hair was wrong. The body wrong, but the face called up a memory from deep within his lizard-like brain. *Where? When? Who?*

"Shit!" His loud profanity drew the attention of the three other customers plus the waitress, manager and cook. Ed couldn't see the six sets of eyes fixed on him as he stared out the window. The man behind the cash register walked over to the stranger. Hearing the footsteps, Ed thought fast.

"I think that little gal might be my cousin, Agnes," Ed said, still staring out the window at Millie.

"That's Millie Lagomarsino. She clerks next door and her husband Duano works on the station. She ain't your cousin Agnes. Now I appreciate your business, but you need to leave."

Ed got up and left the diner. He had other plans and needed to be sure that the young, willowy blonde whom he'd paid for so long ago at Madam Della's was the same person as the pregnant redhead next door. His focus was now beyond curiosity. The humiliation of losing his power and control to a whore fueled his desire for revenge.

His truck sat unmoved as Ed went into the tavern. All he had to say to the lone bartender was "Beer." What kind of beer didn't particularly matter. He took a stool at the corner of the bar nearest the door. How long he might have to wait wasn't important. All that mattered was determining if she was the bitch who tried to cut him. He'd stay, watching the street through the window for a confirming look.

Through the gloom of the bar's perpetual twilight, he counted six other drinkers. Some were men his age, some older, some younger, but all clad in work clothes and boots. Hoping to ingratiate himself, Ed loudly turned a sham question into his type of joke.

"Barkeep, since this here place is 'No Reservations,' do you know what you have if you get six Indians together?" Undaunted by being ignored, Ed shared his punch line. "A full set of teeth," and he guffawed and slapped the countertop at his own hilarity. No one else laughed.

At the far end of the bar, one drinker emerged from the gloom and strode over to the unknown stranger. When a big hand appeared on the bar top Ed turned, smiling as he waited for affirmation from a kindred spirit. The second big hand came to rest on Ed's shoulder and squeezed as the man spoke.

"My wife's an Indian, friend. Why don't you shut the fuck up before I knock you off that stool."

Long ago gone to seed, Ed's only exercise these days came from beating up women and lifting a beer glass. "Sorry Mister, I'm going."

Not wanting to risk missing his target on her way back home, he walked across the street and stopped outside the store. *I could have beaten the shit out of that brush ape if I wanted.*

Pretending to study the window displays, he peeked inside without revealing himself to Millie. Different hair color on top now, but the red matched his memory of the whore's crotch. An evil anticipatory grin spread on his face. He turned back and crossed the street to his truck, now with fantasies of sweet revenge filling his mind.

Still skulking in his truck, Ed saw Millie appear in his rearview mirror when she left the store at 5:00 PM. His lingering anger with the whore who'd defied him was magnified by the recent humiliation in the tavern. He watched as she entered her home. "*NOW,*" he thought as he climbed down from his truck and knocked on her door.

"Yes?" She said to the stranger on her doorstep. "Can I help you?"

Uninvited, he leaned his bulk onto the door frame, blocking closure.

She stepped back inside. "Get the hell out of my house this instant!"

But Ed didn't move as he smiled his evil greeting.

"Hello, Red. Don't you remember me from the whorehouse in Dorris? I think you might want to invite me in to talk about what you owe me."

Shock and surprise left her temporarily speechless, but she stepped back, allowing him entry.

"Thanks, that's nice of you. A lot nicer than when you tried to cut my dick off. Remember me now?"

"What do you want," she hissed.

"Well now, that depends on what you want, little lady. For instance, do you prefer me to wait outside for your husband to come home? Or do you want me to go to the tavern? I could ask all them fellas if anyone knows what the whore four houses down charges." Ed leered at her and shut the front door.

"Maybe you want me to keep your secret? How would that be? Better than the other two choices isn't it?"

As her face flushed with anger and shame, she dropped her gaze. "Keep the secret. Please."

"I can do that, but it will cost you. I'm guessing that you already figured that out?

"Yes."

"OK then. Here's the deal. I don't spill the beans on your whorehouse days. You make it up to me for your bad manners in Dorris. Let's say at a dollar a throw and I've got a five-dollar credit. After that we're square. Have we got a deal?"

Tears were falling as Millie nodded, 'Yes'. She turned off the television in the corner of the room. Arthur Godfrey's round face disappeared as the picture faded from the green screen.

"What time does your baby's daddy get home?"

She whispered back, "6:30."

"Just so you know I'm a gentleman, seeing you're all bumped-up, I'll leave your ass alone for now." Ed stepped across the living room and pulled shut the curtains. Standing in the fading light, he unzipped his fly. "Come and get it, bitch."

When Ed had gone, she tried to make it the bathroom before puking, but didn't. Duano found her, still on her knees, cleaning up vomit. Millie passed off the tears and mess as just part of pregnancy's hormonal cocktail.

16.   Bayview Summer 1952

In Bayview, Eleanor used her 'El' persona of a rich dilettante wannabe writer who lived at the edge of town. Every afternoon she walked along the lakeshore from her rented cabin. El had favorite spots to sit. She could happily do nothing or read as her feet dangled in the waters of Lake Pend Oreille.

The summer heat was in sharp contrast to the cold water surrounding her bare feet as she sat quietly, her back against a red fir tree.

Millie walked right past El without turning her head, apparently unaware of her surroundings.

What can she be doing?

The pregnant redhead was filling her pockets with rocks.

Why? El watched, motionless from her seat a few yards away as the young woman flopped down on the beach crying. El could hear the stranger's sobs, but neither woman moved.

When Millie stood up and stepped to the water's edge, El knew what was about to happen. She was up in an instant. She grabbed Millie by the shoulders a second before her fatal final step into the water. Even one step off the shore would put Millie in water 20 feet deep.

Millie didn't resist El's grasp. She was awake and standing but nothing more. Her mind had turned off the second she'd made the decision to die. She hadn't used the straight razor on herself. Now that she had a house of her own, she didn't want to leave a mess.

El pulled Millie away from the water's edge and forced her to a seat on the small berm behind the shore. Once they were sitting side by side, El's grip relaxed from controlling to hugging.

"Millie, I can't let you take your life. You are too young, pretty, and pregnant to die," El whispered into her ear. "It's me, El. We met in town, at the store. Do you remember?" She got no response. *She is still lost somewhere inside herself.*

"You must be a survivor, like me. Tell me why this? Are you worried about your baby? Is something wrong at home?" The questions hung unanswered for long moments.

Millie's spirit, as a new bride burning bright, had faded when she knelt before Ed, and now it was barely a flicker. "When I'm dead, nothing will hurt anymore."

"All right Millie, can you tell me about your pains? What hurts now? I've known much pain myself, but I survived. Maybe I can help with your pains, so you can survive. Can we try that? Can you trust me that much, girl to girl?"

They sat while Millie decided about sharing such personal pain with this relative stranger. Sensing reluctance, El decided to show her trust in Millie by sharing some of her own secrets.

"Here is part of my pain," and she gave a squeeze to Millie's shoulders. "The Nazis sent my family to Auschwitz, a death camp in Poland. They gassed my parents and starved my brother to death when his use as a slave was done. They used me too as another slave, but I was young, soft and pretty. So, they used me for their sick pleasures." Then El paused as her own composure faltered.

"But I survived. Today I'm strong and no man uses me." El paused again, considering what to say next. "If your pains and troubles are worse than mine, I'll fill my pockets with rocks, and we'll go together."

Minutes passed before Millie's mind came back to the here and now. She turned her head, searching El's face for clues.

"I have a secret from my husband. A man from my past has come back. He threatens to tell my secret if I don't do what he wants. I can't tell my husband because the secret is about the 'me' I used to be, and not the woman he thinks he married. Who I am and who I was are totally different."

El didn't speak. Instead she smiled and gave the shoulder another squeeze.

"It's OK, I understand about secrets. I've shared one of mine with you; a trade, yes? I'll share another one with you. I'm going to find and kill the man who raped and sodomized me."

Millie brushed the tears from her eyes and reached out, taking El's other hand. She was being trusted with something so secret that it could cost El her freedom, if not her life.

"I ran away from home down in Oregon and ended up working in a whorehouse. I sold myself for five dollars a throw. The man who's found me here had paid for me back then. When he wanted what I wouldn't willingly do, he turned me over and tried to stick it in my back door."

"Sodomize you."

"Yes, I was a whore, but I still had some tatters of my self-respect. I wouldn't do that.

"I kept a straight razor under my pillow and was about to cut his filthy dick off. My screams brought the Madam with her ax handle. She smacked him and threw his fat ass out." Again, Millie searched El's face for signs of judgement or revulsion at whom she'd revealed herself to have been.

"You did what you had to do to survive. " El squeezed her hand.

"I stayed with Madam Della's because I had no other place to go. Then one evening a different kind of man came along. He didn't want my body, not at any price. He listened to me and must have seen something there. Pat was his name, and he offered me a way out. I don't know why he did what he did.

"Pat gave me money and clothes and pointed me toward his friends at a place called Keyport, Washington. He put me on a bus with a letter. He saved my life. I changed my name and lied about my history when I got to Keyport. I fell in love with his former roommate, and we're married now. My Duano works at the Bayview station. He doesn't know about my past." Millie stopped talking as she began to tear up. She waited until her composure returned.

"He loves who I became. But he might not love me if he knew who I was."

"I understand." Withdrawing her hand from Millie's grip, El brushed away tears that were about to fall. The two sat in silence until El thought it safe to continue. *She loves her husband. This isn't about hating her rapist but protecting her husband. She needs help.* El's training began to click in.

"Can you tell me about the man? How did he find you here?"

"He's a trucker, and he saw me on the street after making a delivery to Bayview. He says that I owe him and unless I let him do what he wants, he'll tell Duano or tell everyone in the bar who I was and what I used to do."

El listened and finally stood up, offering Millie her hand. "Let's get those rocks out of your pockets." They stood together and looked out across the lake.

"If you promise not to hurt yourself, I'll help you with this problem. I have some experience with men who are problems. Can you do that? Make that promise?"

Millie again searched El's face for affirmation that she could understand and would help. Millie saw what she needed, writ large by the set of El's mouth and the sadness in her eyes.

"Yes."

"All right, now we dump those rocks. Then I need you to write down for me all you can about this man. Whatever you can remember about him will help. Describe him and describe the truck. What you know about his delivery schedule? The days and times he comes. When will he come next? Where does he take you?"

Millie nodded her understanding.

"Come on now, we should go back to Bayview."

Hand in hand they walked. As they passed El's rented cottage, she pointed it out.

"Leave me your notes by sliding them under the front door. When my plan is complete, I'll put the flowerpots from the deck down onto those two front steps as a signal. When you see that, we'll meet again at the place we met today. Agreed?"

Millie nodded, 'Yes,' as they parted, each to her own home.

* * * *

Millie worked late into the night after Duano fell asleep. Everything she knew about 'Ed the Blackmailer' went down on paper. He came to town every third week on a regular haul out of Seattle. So far she'd suffered under him twice, enduring forced oral sodomy.

The full page of notes arrived under El's front door the next day. *I need to help this little one. Maybe that will help me too, or at least earn me one day a year out of hell.*

Two days after she stopped Millie's suicide, she was ready. She placed the flowerpot signal down on the steps. Under one anchoring pot, she left a note: '3:00 meeting today.'

El waved in greeting as Millie came into view on the lakeshore trail. She had a plan but first she had two crucial questions. "Do you hate this man enough to kill him?"

"Of course, I hate him, but this isn't about hate. He threatened my family. Do you see any other way?"

"Can you survive one more visit from the monster?"

Reluctantly, Millie said she would if it had to be. Then El explained her plan. In four days' time, Ed would be back to spend another dollar of his credit. This next visit would be his last.

* * * *

Ed had her right where he wanted. *She really thought that five pieces of ass was all she had to put out, the dumb bitch.* He'd never be done with her. Today would be good. Pregnant or not, today would be a doggie style back door surprise.

His delivery to Bayview done, he parked his truck off the main drag and walked to her door. Taped to the doorknob was a note reading, "*In the park, bring note.*"

"Shit, that bitch. What does she think I am, the delivery boy?"

Ed found her sitting on a bench behind the flagpole and gazebo. "Extra walking pisses me off. This better be good."

"My husband is home sick. Did you take the note off the knob?"

Ed showed her the note before dumping it in a nearby trash can. "So, you're going to do me right here?"

"I know a private place, if we can drive there. Please don't be mad at me."

"All right missy, don't get all worked up. I like you nice and relaxed."

Millie's little bit of begging kept his guard down. "I brought a blanket and some beers." She gestured down to the small chest resting at her feet. "Please, can we just go before somebody sees us?"

"All right, I'll drive the truck up behind the park and you get in there. Where the hell are we going, anyway?"

"Spirit Lake," was the reply.

* * * *

Millie directed Ed to the roadside turn-out on Spirit Lake's south shore. El had hidden an aluminum rowboat in the brush near the small beach. She knew the spot well and was already in her hiding place.

"We're here," Millie told Ed as the wide turn-out came into view. He pulled the truck in and stopped.

"I'll take the blanket down to the beach. There's a nice private spot there. Please bring down the cooler with our beers." When Ed made no protest besides his usual grunts, Millie climbed down from the truck's cab and walked away.

He watched her go. He'd have one beer now and another, maybe hers too, after he'd finished with her. He was still in the driver's seat, looking around at the setting. With one hand Ed opened the cooler lid and reached in for his first beer. A thought crossed his mind. *This isn't very God-damned cold*, an instant before both of the baby rattlesnakes sank their fangs into his hand.

Screaming now, Ed violently shook his hand trying to dislodge the two rattlers. It didn't work. One snake was anchored to the skin between his thumb and forefinger. The other rattler bit into the flesh of his palm just above his pinkie.

Ed had no words, only screams when he exited the truck and began waving his arm, striking the snakes against the truck. Both snakes died as Ed whipped them repeatedly against the fender. Still, the two 12-inch bloody ribbons of snake body wouldn't release their hold on the trucker's hand.

As El and Millie watched, Ed attempted to shed the snakes. He grabbed one of the intact snake heads in his free hand and used his thumb to pry it off. It worked! Unfortunately, the dead reptile's head operated on its own and bit into his thumb. Wild with pain and unable to escape the fangs, he felt the three doses of venom coursing through his body. Ed's screaming continued right up to the moment when, in his blurred vision and unimaginable pain, he collided with a large red fir tree.

When the unconscious Ed slumped to the ground, they sprang into action. El dragged his body down to the lakeshore while Millie taped a prepared note to the steering wheel. The note, short and concise, suggested that fat Ed had removed himself from the truck driving game.

"I quit this shit," was all it said. With the note in place, she checked the cab for any trace of herself. Finding none, she closed the driver's side door and joined El and the unconscious Ed at the lakeshore.

Millie brought out her straight razor from its hiding place. Then she uttered only one word to El. "Now?"

El nodded. "Now."

Millie's long contained white-hot rage blurred her vision as the blade bit into his throat. Ed would soon achieve his highest, best and most evolved purpose: fish food.

His twice-bitten right hand and once-bitten left thumb had both started to turn black. El stripped his body and made strategic cuts to insure it would not float to the surface. Together they dragged his corpse into the water, leaving a small trail of blood smearing the sand. They attached it to the skiff. El knew that the corpse would soon lose sphincter control and become even more foul smelling in death than Ed had been in life.

"Where did you get the snakes?"

"They live in a rock pile up behind my cabin. I watched the den and when they emerged, I pinned them with a forked stick, then tossed them into a canvas sack. I chose two babies since they are the most poisonous. I set the sack of snakes in my refrigerator and they fell asleep. They warmed up inside the empty cooler and waited silently for an opportunity to take revenge."

"Millie, take my car and go home. The keys are on top of the right front tire. I'll walk back after fatso goes for his swim. You're free now."

Millie grabbed El in as much of an embrace as her belly allowed. After the hug, El saw the light in her new friend's eyes. *She's relieved. She's free to be a Mommy. She doesn't get any satisfaction from killing, just peace. I could use some of that.*

El waited for full dark before she paddled to the deep water over the Spirit Lake sink hole. Pulling the slightly submerged body to the side of her skiff, she cut the tow line and Ed slipped away under the warm green water to join Randall in a long, dreamless sleep.

By moonlight El cleaned any traces of blood from the skiff with lake water and returned the boat to its rightful place by the last cabin at the Shady Rest Resort.

17. Birth

Millie's night was far from over. Ten minutes into the drive home her water broke. She had no time to think and began driving south to the hospital in Coeur d' Alene. When her first contraction arrived, she momentarily lost focus and just missed colliding with a northbound logging truck. With that lesson learned, she slowed down to a 20-mile-per-hour clip and pulled off the road whenever the contractions returned.

The Emergency Room staff placed a call to Duano announcing her whereabouts and condition. Then Millie asked to talk to him.

"You're about to be a daddy, darling. There just wasn't time for a note. I guess your wife is a car thief now, too. I borrowed El's car and drove."

"As long as you're OK, I forgive you. How are you feeling?"

Duano got his answer in the form of a series of loud cries. "Ow-ow-ow. Get here! Ow-ow-ow."

The next voice on the line was a nurse. "Your wife is going into the delivery room. Leave home now." Duano made the drive in record time, but not fast enough to beat the arrival of his daughter.

Millie thanked God for two miracles that day, the birth of a healthy child and the end of Ed. She insisted they name the infant Ellen Rose; because of Ellen Ripley's car, she explained, and in honor of her own mother. They'd call the baby Rosie.

As they sat together with their daughter, he brought out a small box from the pocket of his Filson jacket. Inside she found a custom-made gold and ruby cigar-band-shaped ring, exactly matching the paper band that had initially signaled their engagement back on VJ Day.

Duano took the ring from the box and removed the weathered paper cigar band from her left hand. He slipped its replacement on Millie's ring finger and leaned over to kiss her.

"I love you babe," was all he said, and they hugged as best they could while Rosie nursed.

* * * *

El became a close friend to the Lagomarsino family and remained Millie's confidant. Her own tears fell when she found out the baby girl's name. For a more tangible show of appreciation, they took El to dinner at Luigi's.

They were greeted at the restaurant door by Vince. Duano shook the maître d's hand.

"Vince, this is our special friend Ellen Ripley. She is our guest tonight, and I'd like her to be a special friend of the house whenever she comes in."

Next, Millie took El by the hand and walked her the kitchen's swinging doors. She pointed to Chef Frank whose back was visible as he worked multiple hot pans on the big eight-burner restaurant stove. "Frank, it's me, Millie."

"Hi Mil." Frank raised one hand in recognition but continued attending to his pans. When Frank turned to plate up his creation, she spoke again. "This is my friend, Ellen. I wanted her to meet the artist who is cooking our dinner."

"Hi," was all the man of few words added.

Taking the hint, they returned to the dining room. Brizzalera's massive figure loomed over Duano, who was now seated at their table for the evening. He had already told the giant about baby Rosie and how El had helped Millie when she went into labor.

Brizz tipped his head and kissed the back of El's offered hand. His gentle and refined manners, along with the immaculate tuxedo, belied the giant's capacity for violence. As the meal was ending, Chef Frank appeared at the table, in his hand a bottle of grappino, the water-clear, fiery brandy found in most Italian homes. Frank poured the liquor into four glasses that arrived from the bar. The silent chef nodded in appreciation of their multiple compliments about his cooking.

Frank was a teapot of a man, cool on the outside but hot on the inside. His eyes lingered on El as the four shared a toast. His lingering glance and smile were returned.

* * * *

This first dinner became one of many for Frank and El. As the month progressed, so did their relationship, from dinners at the Lagomarsinos' home, to dinners at El's cabin and then just the two of them having dinners alone at Frank's.

She lingered for 'another drink' when Duano and Millie excused themselves after a dinner at Luigi's. After one more drink, Frank drove El home. It was in her bed and by her choice, that they first made love. Both silent by nature, their shared intimacy over time turned their pillow talk to the deepest, most personal kind.

Frank told her about the demons that haunted his sleep. In slow, halting sentences he tried to explain how he had killed any Japanese in front of him, including the women and children. With his narrative over, he silently stared up at the bedroom ceiling.

El freed herself from the warmth of his side and sat back against the headboard. She showed him the six-number tattoo on the inside of her left wrist. He held her as she cried and, in painful detail, spilled out the rest of her story about Auschwitz.

"I'm scared."

"Why? What scares you, the demons?"

First came a shake of her head. "No, I'm scared that I'll lose you, if you know the full truth."

Frank replied with his own slow head shake.

"There's more I have to tell you because you have a right to know. More important, you need to know who I am and what I've done. The risk of loving someone is the other side of trusting them with who we really are."

Frank moved his gaze from the ceiling to his love's face, and he listened.

"I killed people. After the war I trained as an assassin in Israel. I was part of a team that killed Nazis war criminals we'd hunted down. My last kill was in New York and then I left the group," and she paused, "but not the killing." Frank squeezed her hand as they lay side by side in the filtered moonlight reflecting off the lake.

"I've killed after that, and it was a hired killing that brought me to Idaho. I still take jobs but now with you I don't want to do what I've done any more." Again, she paused. "You showed me yours, so now I've showed you mine."

18.   Bayview 1953

Dr. Werner Kleinheintz was respected at work and comfortable in his Coeur d' Alene lakeshore home. He set his own hours at Bayview. The half-hour drive from home to office, traversed in the leather seat of his Mercedes 500 sedan, was a beautiful interlude. Comfortable in his surroundings, he lunched in Bayview, Athol or Coeur d'Alene as he pleased. Time was not his master.

It was at a simple lunch in Bayview when the Doktor materialized in front of El. She was now the dilettante, wannabe travel writer, Ellen Ripley. With a love now in her life, she was committed to stepping away from her former life as a contract killer. But exacting revenge on Werner Kleinheintz, her abuser, was a different matter.

They were both ten years older. Her maturity and a different haircut and color all made her less recognizable to him. El knew the person seated across the room was Dr. Werner Kleinheintz, the man who had raped and sodomized her for years. She lingered over her plate, allowing him to leave so she could follow him. Her hunt had begun.

El had a lot to plan. If she could handle Werner away from Bayview, it would both ease dealing with a body and keep a separation between Bayview and her kill site. Her plan formed around luring him to a chosen killing field. But how?

A letter, she decided. She'd use her New York contacts to forward a letter to reconnect with the man she intended to kill. It had to show a tortured path from Eleanor to Werner, and the physical appearance of the letter was the key.

Dearest Werner,

I've never forgotten our promises to find each other after the war. I spent a year in a Displaced Persons camp in Germany. Then with the help of international organizations they lined me up with a sponsor in the United States. I came to America in the fall of 1949, first to St. Louis where my sponsor lived. In 1951 I found a job as a nanny for a couple living in the small resort town of Spirit Lake, Idaho. This place is so clean and beautiful after all we had seen, that I've stayed. Here is my address, if you ever receive this letter. I fear it may never reach you because where you are is unknown to me. So, I do what I can and what my love for you demands of me.

With love and hope,

Eleanor

The note was back dated to October 31, 1951. While written by El, its provenance and delivery route were as contrived as the sentiment. Her DIN and mob contacts included forgers and corrupt postal employees. It was essential that when her final product got to Werner, he believed it had reached him almost accidentally through the anonymous US government bureaucracy. Her envelope's travels would be witnessed by its multiple forwarding annotations and its final arrival as an envelope inside an envelope. If her ruse convinced Werner the rapist that, by the barest of coincidences, his lost love had found him, he'd come to her. When he did, his heart full of lust, Eleanor would kill him.

The New York forger enlisted to age her love note appropriately told her when the letter went out. With mob help, the bait letter entered postal channels at

Spokane. A crooked mail clerk who made a business of selling "stop delivery" dates to local burglars added the final rerouting stamps and passed it along to Bayview. The note showed her newly rented Spirit Lake Post Office box for a return address.

Eleanor was a patient huntress. She put out the word that she was not taking any new contracts. She'd watch, wait and plan until her molester was a sure kill. She began daily checks of her post office box, hoping for a sign that Werner had taken the bait. Eleanor was a promise keeper. "I'll find you," were her parting words; that was a promise she intended to carry out.

While she waited for the bait letter to hook this bottom feeding, scum sucker of a man, she researched her target and planned. Where did Werner live? Where did he work? Did he have a car and, if so, what did it look like? What were his routine arrival and departure times? All these were things she needed to find out to plan her attack.

Her research began outside the same luncheonette in Bayview where she saw him for the first time since Auschwitz. Eleanor chose a park bench in the Bayview City Park. The bench farthest from the street gave her a wide field of view, from the station gate to past the diner and off to the north end of town. Her chosen surveillance time was one hour before lunch to see if he had a routine she could discern. And he did.

Eleanor determined that Herr Doktor Werner sometimes lunched at the Bayview Diner. He came from the research station and returned there. Now she knew where he worked.

Next she changed her surveillance to 4:00 P.M. Her new viewing spot was opposite the research station's main gate. She hoped to see him leaving work, to know his regular departure time.

Herr Doktor was a man of routine. He drove out the gate every weekday between 4:30 and 5:00 P.M., saluting the guards as he passed. His gold-colored Mercedes sedan was a virtual one-of-a-kind in northern Idaho. Now she knew his car and departure time. His arrival at work no longer mattered.

Eleanor needed to follow the good doctor as he left Bayview on the one road leading out of town. With his departure time and vehicle known, she changed her surveillance accordingly. Her new spot would be off the Bayview road where it connected with Highway 95. At 4:00 P.M. she took up her chosen post across the highway intersection, parking in the lot of a laundromat. She had only to watch and wait. Did he head south or north? When he arrived, Werner turned south towards Coeur d'Alene.

Next, Eleanor planned to follow Werner as he drove south. North of the intersection was Schooney's Diner, her new starting point. She'd pull out of the lot and onto the highway, just another anonymous car, when the big Mercedes came into view. From a few car-lengths back, his travel could be tracked all or partway home. Perhaps another surveillance trip would be necessary if other cars stopped providing her cover. It didn't matter because each successive trip put her closer to revenge.

As a man who valued order, Werner arrived at the intersection of the Bayview Road and Highway 95 at 5:10 P.M. *Right on schedule*, smiled El. She eased out of Schooney's parking lot and fell in behind the big Mercedes as it headed south towards Coeur d' Alene. Relying on her DIN training, Eleanor stayed two to three cars behind the gold sedan. She followed him south through the small town of Hayden Lake and into a suburban area of Coeur d' Alene. When his route into the neighborhood separated him from the cars she'd hidden behind, Eleanor turned right when he turned left onto Lincoln Street. She pulled over and stopped. After a five-minute break she slowly reversed her route, noting the intersection and where and when she'd broken off the pursuit.

She chose her next interception point. She'd wait, parked one block down from where they'd separated today. Here she would watch and wait for her quarry to pass. If Werner drove the same route tomorrow, she'd follow him farther on his drive home. Maybe he would go to his house tomorrow, maybe not; it didn't matter. If Werner didn't reappear at the same spot where they'd parted, she'd follow him again from Schooney's back in Athol. Eleanor already knew his fate. She was just choosing the place of his execution.

The drive from Bayview to Coeur d' Alene had taken Werner 35 minutes, so she'd be in place 30 minutes before his expected arrival.

Snug in the comforts of the new country that needed his help, Werner arrived within five minutes of yesterday's time. When he turned left onto Lincoln Street, she pulled out, crossed the intersection, and followed his Mercedes from a block behind. *Don't scare him now!*

Soon the hunted and hunter were passing through long blocks of stores and restaurants. When they turned back into a residential neighborhood, Eleanor found herself along the Coeur d' Alene Lake shore. Still well back, she slowed and pulled into a parking lot as Werner's car came to rest in front of a tidy craftsman bungalow. "Tubb's Hill Park" read the large wooden sign across the lot from where she sat.

Eleanor took a moment to get oriented. His was the third house from the corner and painted a soft blue. Choosing a hard-packed dirt path into the tall trees of the park, she paralleled the street to see if a safe view of his house and yard presented themselves. El found the spot she wanted in a tree-covered rise above and behind the house.

A large picture window provided a panoramic view of the lake and Tubb's Hill. A single half-glass door gave access from what looked like his living room to a large wooden deck that stopped just feet away from the gravel beach.

Twenty minutes had passed when Werner emerged onto the deck, his gabardine slacks and shirt now replaced by black swim trunks. He sat down on the edge of the deck, a tall glass in one hand.

Eleanor appraised Werner's body as a boxer sizes up an opponent. A soft roll of fat around his middle ballooned the waistband of his trunks. His arms were not thin, but neither were they well muscled.

Werner got up and walked into the shallows and then dove into the lake. This was her chance to get a closer look at the house.

Hurrying back down the path to the parking lot past her car, Eleanor strolled along his street. She stopped to smell the flowers in street-side gardens, noting house numbers and checking for names on mailboxes or by front doors as she went. At the far corner of Werner's block, she crossed the street and headed back to her car at the same casual pace. She was just another tourist admiring the lifestyle of the lakefront dwellers.

Driving back to Bayview, Eleanor thought over what she now knew: his hours, routine, car, address and the softness of his body. Now she must wait for Werner to take her bait.

* * * *

The letter found its way to Herr Doktor Werner Kleinheintz. The forged stamping and handwritten routing directions seemed to vouch for its tortured path and pedigree: almost eighteen months enroute from the initial mailing to:

Doctor Werner Kleinheintz,

C/O War Department,

Washington, D.C.

Through many hands and across many desks, the trail of stampings and annotations led to the Navy and then to Bayview. Reading the note, Werner thought about the young Jewess. He remembered his promise to her. *Did I love her then? Perhaps I did, at least enough to spare her life.*

But now, here she was, and so temptingly close. He placed the letter in a desk drawer and went to the men's lavatory. Locking himself in a stall, he masturbated as he recalled her body and her wonderful compliant nature. Aha! *How could she not love me, the little Jew. If her lips remain as pink, I might still enjoy her.*

He fancied himself to be her savior again. He could save her from poverty, work or normalcy, and invite her into his life of honor and privilege, if she was still so compliant. The return address was a box number, so he'd have to be content with sweet memories for now. He wrote back that night.

Dearest Eleanor,

I feared you were lost to me forever. And here you are, and so close to me! *Gott* must want us together because we are only miles apart, my darling. I work for the winners now at Bayview, which is near you. Here is my address in Coeur d' Alene. Come to me, my darling. If you are without means or transportation, I will come to you. Please write soon.

Love, Werner

* * * *

Standing outside the small post office at Spirit Lake with his letter in hand, her next move was long planned. Eleanor had her response waiting.

Dearest Werner,

My beloved savior, I cried with joy when I read your words. I have so much to tell and so much lost time to make up for. I am here, living with sponsors. I work as their nanny for two brats, so I have little time and less privacy. I don't have any car and get paid very little beyond room and board. If you can send me money, I could rent a bungalow by our small lake for a private reunion when the brats are asleep? I so miss your big German sausage.

Love you, my sweet,

Eleanor

"The little Jew bitch wants money now," cursed Werner as he read her note. "I gave her life, food, a roof. But so what? With Jews, everything is for sale, including her body." His complaints were spoken to the trees where Tubb's Hill Park stopped, and the lakeshore began. "So, I'll pay, at least once. It's no matter." With that, he walked back inside his bungalow and composed his response.

> My dear little girl,
> Yes, we need to meet. I will come for you when you say, after our love nest is arranged. It tortures me every moment that we're still apart. Do it soon, my love.
> Werner

He enclosed two twenty-dollar bills with his message. As he licked the envelope flap, it crossed his mind, *Or maybe I should kill her? She presents an unseemly part of my past. What fun; I could do both!*

Her reply reached Werner one week later.

> Darling Werner,
> I have our special place. The Edgewater Resort is on the north shore of Spirit Lake. There are ten guest cabins. I'll be waiting inside one for you. You will know where I am by the red sweater I'll leave on the porch. I can arrange it for ten days from now. That gives you time to tell me if the date and place are not good. If I don't hear from you, I'll be waiting for you. Remember to bring your swimming trunks!
> Eleanor

The date and place of his death were now known to his executioner.

* * * *

The bungalow was rented in Werner's name via a phone call to the resort. The rental fee for the cabin followed in a letter. Eleanor had requested the cabin that would work best. From her private arsenal, she assembled everything necessary to do the job.

Werner arrived at the appointed hour and parked the big Mercedes in the gravel space beside the cabin marked with the red sweater. He had brought his own kit: swim trunks, condoms, a ball gag and a small whip. The kit also included a short-barreled pistol, in case Werner found Eleanor not to his liking after all these years.

Stepping onto the cabin's porch, he tapped at the door. It opened in response. There she stood, naked before him and surely wet with anticipation!

Summoning all her strength, she fought off the nausea his touch and kiss brought. Eleanor didn't speak; she stepped into his embrace, drawing him inside. Werner closed the door behind them.

He kissed her roughly and lifted the delicate body onto the double bed.

"I want to look at you," he said. Standing above Eleanor's form, he methodically scanned her small breasts. His hand went to a nipple, and he squeezed. She wanted to cry out. Instead, she responded with a smile. His other hand traced a path down her body to her pubis, which she had shaved. *The better to look like a little girl again to lure this pig.*

El watched his eyes as he continued to scan her body. She heard the small changes in his breathing as his gazed returned to just above her smooth thighs. He liked what he saw; she had not become unattractive to him.

Eleanor closed her eyes and waited as Werner slowly undressed. She posed with hands behind her head, adding to the image of vulnerability she intended. Her right hand clutched a leather-covered sap. She'd only have to endure his touch for a little while longer. Naked now, Werner began to descend, his body covering hers.

"Darling, please may I be on top this time?" she purred. "I want you to see my face as I make love to you." The Doktor found nothing wrong in her plea and he rolled off her and lay by her side. Eleanor began to rise as her hands came down to her sides. Then came a swift kiss from the leather-covered sap to his temple.

Eleanor rummaged through his toy chest and found the gun. *He was going to eliminate a link to his perverted past unless he found me to be the same willing victim that he'd left at Auschwitz.* She removed the gun for her own later use and took out the swim trunks and ball gag. She slid his trunks up his legs and over the fading erection. The gag went into his mouth.

Werner was unconscious and Eleanor set about binding him. First she wrapped his wrists with wash cloths from the cabin. Then she tied his wrists together behind his back, using strong cord. Finally, she did the same binding to his ankles, using bathroom towels. There could be no bruises or other marks suggesting that he had been bound.

Then she dressed and waited for Werner to wake up. As his eyes began to focus, he became aware that he could not command his limbs to move.

Eleanor stood at the bedside. "Werner, I want you to see who's killing you. It's me, the little Jew who you sodomized. Hear my words, from the same mouth where you forced your schwantz." Leaning over her prey, she spat in his face.

"You are going to die tonight. But you have a choice. You can have a quick and easy death or a slow, painful one. The choice is yours, but the price of an easy passing is telling me where more of your kind are hiding. If you give me two names and places, then you'll die in your sleep, in this soft bed from a drug overdose. Do you understand?"

As she spoke, Eleanor held up a series of tools for her captive to study and imagine their use: a sharp knife, a small saw and a butane cigarette lighter.

Speaking was impossible with the ball gag in his mouth, but still he tried to grunt a "Yes."

"Good. I will take the gag out of your mouth now. If you scream, the gag goes back in and you get to feel and smell your burning schwantz. Will you be quiet for me?"

Again he managed an affirmative grunt.

After Werner gave up Schwarz and Schnabel's location, Eleanor added, "If you lie to me about any of this, I'll be back with my toys. I will check your information and then be back. When you piss yourself, think of me." Then she put the gag back in his mouth.

* * * *

She drove to the church compound on the rim rock above Hayden Lake. At the wooden gate Eleanor got out of her car and stood waiting for someone inside the compound to appear. A large man in khaki work clothes approached.

"Can I help you?"

"Yes please. I'm Elsa, Dr. Kleinheintz's secretary. I have a private message for Hans and Hubert. Are they available?"

"They are here, yes, but off working now. Can I pass the message for you?"

"No, thank you. My instructions are to tell those two, but no one else. Do you know when they might return? I will come back."

"Sorry I can't help with that."

"No problem, I will try again later," and Eleanor got back into her car and returned to Spirit Lake.

* * * *

Sticking to her plan, she parked again at the view spot outside of the resort where Werner was held. A short walk through the trees brought her back to the rented bungalow.

Twilight had darkened the resort grounds. Inside, Werner was still in the same spot, lying motionless and gagged.

"Your information was correct. You've earned an easy death. I will change into my swimsuit and then we're going for a boat ride and a swim. We'll both feel better."

Werner's eyes widened in terror as the promised peaceful death came into question. A swim and a boat ride? What was this? Where was the easy death?

Eleanor reappeared in a bathing suit and eased Werner from the bed to the floor. She cradled his head, careful not to bruise his body as she dragged him outside. Each bungalow had its own aluminum boat, beached at water's edge. Werner's legs went in first and then his torso. She pushed the boat off the beach and then climbed in herself.

She rowed the short distance to the spot where Randall Albers rested under 100 feet of water. Werner was not to share Randall's final rest. She carefully scanned the shore for any potential witnesses. Seeing no one, she lifted Werner legs-first into the blood-warm waters of Spirit Lake and then joined him. Eleanor cradled the man's head against her body. Then she pushed his head below the surface and removed the ball gag. Werner first attempted to speak, but no sound came out of the water.

"Werner, I lied, there is no easy death for you." She held him under until water had filled his lungs, and he was gone. She watched his eyes, just below the surface, as his fear left them when he ceased to struggle. Then she untied the bindings and pushed his body away as she swam to shore.

Eleanor dried and dressed. The wet towel and wash cloths that had bound Werner went into the bathtub. She gathered up Werner's bag of toys he'd intended to use on her and checked for any telltale sign that he had not been alone. Finding nothing to tie her to the cabin, Eleanor retraced her steps through the woods to her car. She'd soon be gone.

When his body was found the next day, there'd be no indications of foul play. Werner's name was on the rental. His Mercedes was parked beside the bungalow. An accidental death would not spook the Nazis hiding at the Aryans' church. His death would appear to be just another tragic accident.

* * * *

The Kootenai County Sheriff identified the body and contacted Bayview. The autopsy detected nothing to suggest Kleinheintz's death was anything other than an accident. The Doktor died, perhaps from a muscle cramp as he swam? The bruise on his temple suggested that he'd accidently hit his head on the boat's rail when diving into the lake. No one knew for sure.

It was a Coeur d' Alene newspaper story that alerted Reverend Royce to Werner's passing. Hubert reported Werner's demise to a high-level contact within the *Werwolfs* organization. The work of recruiting *Werwolfs* for the future Fourth Reich had to continue. A replacement for Doktor Kleinheintz would have to be arranged.

19. Further Revenge, 1953

El was now the one who needed Millie's help. At least two more Nazis were hiding at the church compound. She needed a means of access. Could Millie, through her connection to Bonnie, help El get to them? On or off the compound didn't matter to El; she could develop a plan for either circumstance.

When Millie had parenting under control, El raised the subject during a lunch meeting. "Millie, there is more to my story than I've yet shared with you. I must ask a favor, but before I do, you need to know why I'm asking."

Millie put down her sandwich and gave full attention to what was coming.

El recounted the whole tale of the killing of her parents at Auschwitz. "I told you on the day we met at the lakeshore how I hoped to kill the man who'd found me desirable enough to live, as long as I fulfilled his sick fantasies. For two years he used my body as he wished. I hated him then and thought about killing myself. Instead I lived, paying any price for my life. I didn't know then that the Nazis had murdered my entire family, so I lived, hoping to find them someday." She paused, her gaze never moving from Millie's face.

"My abuser, I just killed him." El stopped talking, letting the gravity of her admission register. "After the war I sneaked into Palestine. There I became part of the DIN, partisans and camp survivors who wanted to punish the worst of the Nazis who escaped Allied or Russian justice."

Reaching her hand across the kitchen table, Millie focused on El's face before speaking. "Tell me what you need. I owe you my life and Rosie's life too. I owe you for giving me back peace of mind and saving my marriage."

El took her friend's hand. *My little sister wants to help me with my demons, like I helped her with hers.*

"I need a contact inside the Aryans' church. Two Nazis, Hans Schnabel and Hubert Schwarz, are hiding there. They need to die for what they did at Auschwitz. I know who they are, but I need more information. When and where do they work and sleep? I need to get them outside the church compound. You work with Bonnie and she's the wife of the church leader."

"Yes, I'll help get what you want. I need to think about what to do. I've never been to their compound but Duano has been up there."

The two former victims finished their lunch and separated, Millie to the store and El to her cabin. Both the women now were focusing on the new task at hand.

That night Millie asked Duano about what he knew about the church group. "Since I work with Bonnie, I'm curious about them. I'd like to visit the compound myself. I might find a babysitter there for our Rosie. I don't enjoy having to take her to work with me."

Duano had no problem with his wife's desire to get help with their daughter. While they both steered clear of all things political or religious about the church, individual members could still be friends.

An idea was forming in Millie's mind. Could she use the babysitting ploy to get El's Nazis out from the safety of their compound? The next day at work she presented a sanitized sketch of the childcare idea to Bonnie. They explored the idea whenever the store was not busy.

Bonnie said she would need to get her husband's permission.

Millie nodded. "I need to see where Rosie would be and meet the sitter. It's the Mommy gene in me coming out."

* * * *

El and Millie met for lunch three times per week. At their next meeting, Millie shared what she'd done so far. El considered how Millie's idea could be bent to her own use.

"If you could work a deal where you drive Rosie to the compound in the mornings, ask if they can bring her back here at night. Offer them more money for the service. I'll pay. Explain that you need to make dinner and do housekeeping things in the evening,"

Reverend Royce gave Bonnie permission to bring Millie up for a tour of the church compound. She'd see the nursery space and meet the sitter. Her visit was arranged for the following Sunday. Bonnie's store was closed that day, so she was free to play tour guide.

Arriving at the church compound on Sunday, Millie waited outside the locked gate, standing in the shadow of the observation tower. *Why does a church need a wire fence and a guard tower?* Bonnie walked out to meet her as the gate came open. She took Millie by the hand and led her around the compound area before going inside the combination church, office, chapel, and meeting/dining room.

"Here we are, dear." Bonnie pointed to a half-closed Dutch door. "As our congregation grows, we'll need a nursery for ourselves. Let's go in and I'll introduce you to some folks." Stepping through the open door, Millie recognized her other former neighbor, Betty. She had a paint roller in one hand and was wearing an oversized man's shirt as a painting smock.

"Hey kiddo, it's good to see you. Congratulations on little Rosie. I understand the Mommy Bear feelings of motherhood. We feel the same way about protecting our own. I'd hug you if I weren't a human paint rag at the moment."

Millie returned the greeting and smiled. Holding up her roller, Betty explained "We alternate wall colors, first blue then pink. Let me get out of my smock and rinse this roller. I'll catch up with you two in the dining room over coffee."

Bonnie directed Millie to the kitchen and dining area. Two rows of tables filled the center of the room. A cafeteria-style set of steam tables anchored one end of the large room off to her right. To her left along the back wall were two more tables set up as a beverage station. Coffee urn, a hot tea urn, a two-tap refrigerated milk dispenser and a clear plastic reservoir of grape-colored liquid lined the tables. Cups and plastic glasses in neat rows between the four machines completed the tableau. Bonnie gestured to the coffee urn as they approached the two tables.

"Let's get a cup, grab a table and wait for Betty. Betty will be Rosie's sitter. The nursery should be finished in three days."

Millie was delighted to hear that Betty would be Rosie's sitter.

Betty soon joined them at the table. Millie brought up El's idea, concealed in terms of needing to have someone drive Rosie home in the afternoon.

Bonnie and Betty said they'd consider the request. "We have car seats left over from our own kids. There may be times when I wouldn't be the driver," said Betty.

"But don't worry, there are reliable people I trust that could drive her home."

"Hans or Hubert?" asked Bonnie.

Bonnie looked at Betty who nodded in agreement. Next they discussed what the babysitting and driving would cost. Gasoline was not free. Millie offered to cover any expense the extra service caused and to pay for a driver's time.

When it was time for Millie to go, they promised an answer in the next two days. Betty went back to her painting and Bonnie walked Millie to her car. "See you tomorrow, kiddo," Bonnie said as she waved goodbye.

Millie got an answer the next day when Bonnie opened the store. The babysitting price she'd offered was fine as was her second offer concerning bringing Rosie home every day. Betty would drive whenever possible. Her trusted security men, Hans or Hubert, would be her substitutes when necessary. El and Millie's plan was coming together.

* * * *

Over their regular Monday lunch with El, Millie shared what she'd arranged. "We start using the sitter tomorrow. Betty will bring Rosie home. She used to be our neighbor before they moved up there when the reverend opened the church compound. Betty is the reverend's secretary and her husband, Curtis, is the church's printer. Hans and Hubert are the two security guys for the compound. One or the other of them will be Betty's back-up driver."

Listening intently, El asked, "How will we know when either of the Nazis will be driving?"

"I'm not sure we will. I'll ask whoever brings Rosie home if I'll see them again tomorrow. That would give you twenty-four hours to plan. We just have to see how that plays out."

Now it was El's turn to finalize her plan for dealing with the Nazis. She went to the local realtor and extended her lease on the vacation cabin. She now had more reasons to stay than just her love of the area. El knew that the death of Werner had been seen as a tragedy. The death of a second Nazi might be a coincidence, but a third death would ring out as a conspiracy.

El had learned in the DIN that planning was the key to success. She drove the road between Bayview and the church compound to choose her interception point. There was a wide spot at a viewpoint. The timber was sparse there and over the edge of the cliff was a good two-hundred-foot drop.

She chose the scenario for the trap she'd set. A pretty woman stuck on the roadside with car trouble. El had all the supplies she needed, except for a liquid anesthetic for dosing the driver. Her car trouble at the overlook gave her a quick way to dispose of the Nazi's vehicle. The clear, amber oral anesthetic, liberally applied to the Nazi, would complete the tableau of an unfortunate accident.

* * * *

Betty delivered little Rosie home predictably at 5:00 P.M. Sometimes Betty came in for a quick coffee while Millie made dinner. Whether she came to the front door or if Rosie was passed off at curbside, Millie always ended with the same key line, "See you tomorrow." Betty never recognized the innocent comment for the question it was.

El waited for the crucial tip-off that they hoped Betty would unintentionally provide. After a month of routine hand-offs, the answer she'd been waiting for came.

"I've got a dental appointment tomorrow afternoon so one of our security men will be bringing Rosie home. They know what to do and I'll be back in two days."

Millie passed the news to El by putting out on her porch a rainbow flag, an agreed signal that tomorrow El's quarry would pass her way. Since El made daily visits to town, the flag symbol was a secret message hidden in plain sight. El saw the signal flag and already knew a close approximate time for her interception.

* * * *

It was Hans who showed up at the Lagomarsinos' that afternoon as Betty's replacement driver. The big German was an archetypal blond from the Third Reich. Polite but businesslike,

He held the car door open as she removed little Rosie from her car seat. Millie made a point of waiting and waving a goodbye from the curb as he drove off, headed back to the church compound. She didn't know if El had seen the signal flag message. Neither did she know the details of El's plan. But tomorrow she'd find out if the world was a better place because there was one less asshole in Idaho.

El parked at her kill site and raised the hood of her car. To sweeten the trap, she'd dressed in a too-short skirt and too-tight blouse. Her trusty leather sap was stashed on top of the car's right front tire.

Hans Schnabel was passing the roadside viewpoint on his drive back to the church compound when he saw the stranded motorist. El had draped herself over the fender of her car, causing her skirt to ride up deliciously high. When she heard the other vehicle pull onto the gravel of the overlook, she turned towards the arrival. Her cleavage showed as a further attractant while she smoothed down the hem of her skirt. El's face displayed desperation, no smile at her lip line, and big sad eyes, especially created for Hans. As she reeled in her catch, he was unaware that he'd even been hooked.

She faced Hans and at the right moment put a pout on her lips and threw down the soiled towel she'd been holding.

He got out of the car and walked over. "Can I help you?"

"Oh, thank you for stopping. I don't know why it quit. I don't know what to do. If you could look, I'd be very grateful."

He picked up the discarded shop towel as El moved out of his way to her spot on the opposite wheel well.

The big German leaned into the engine compartment. El did the same from across the car, the better to display her cleavage. Her right hand, hidden from his view, reached the sap on her front tire. His head and hands played in the engine compartment as El walked back to his side of the car, the sap invisible behind her back. She had to discipline herself and not take the easy strike at the back of his head. Through tense moments she waited. The blow must be to the front of his head to be believable, as if caused by impact with the steering wheel.

El stood by his side and let her perfume do its work. When Hans turned around, her rosy nipples were close under a thin drape of fabric. With the rise of his head slowed by her assets, she struck the crown of his forehead. Down he went like a pole-axed steer.

El retrieved her bottle of anesthetic — Old Crow Bourbon — and poured a slow stream into the reclining man's mouth. She paused, not wanting to choke the former Auschwitz guard.

Next she drove his car to the viewpoint edge. Still unconscious, Hans got another mouthful of bourbon. When he groaned, another dose of sap was applied to the same spot and out he went again. El wiped her fingerprints from the bottle with a handkerchief and then forced Han's hand onto the glass. She poured the balance of the whiskey on his clothing. Now marked with his prints, the bottle went into the front seat of his car.

El dragged him to the driver's side door. With some struggle, she finally managed to place the big man inside. She started the engine and put the idling car into drive. The engine labored but didn't stall when she released the emergency brake. She watched as the big sedan's front tires rolled over the edge of the viewpoint cliff and stopped.

"SHIT!" The sedan had high-centered on its long steel frame. The rear tires were still spinning, but the angle of the sedan's tilt stripped them of traction.

First El tried pushing from behind. No luck. Next she began rocking the sedan by pushing down on its rear bumper. Again she had no luck.

What to do—what to do, a mantra chanted to herself. Hans had to die on the rocks below the cliff. Then, still in fear of discovery by a passing motorist, El retrieved the jack from her car. As quick as she could, she set it up on the sedan's bumper. Using the tire iron as a handle, El raised the rear bumper enough that gravity finally saved the day and propelled a whisky-soaked Hans on his final ride to the rocks 200 feet below.

El replaced the jack in her trunk before stealing a final look at the wreck below as flames from the engine began to lick towards a ruptured gas tank.

20. Richard, 1953

Millie heard the story of the falling car from El over lunch the next day. "Some poor village is without its asshole," she commented.

"When I dropped the baby off this morning, there were lots of worried looks at the compound because Hans was not back. I said nothing and offered to help in any search they might organize. Betty didn't say anything about problems with our sitting routine."

El had been quiet through their lunch.

"I need you to tell me, when they find out he's dead, if the compound buys the idea that big Hans had a few belts in the car and accidently drove off the cliff. What I do next depends on what the church believes. If they sense a connection between Werner and Hans, then I'll need a new plan to get Hubert."

Millie understood El's thinking. There might be future Nazi victims up there if she was patient and they weren't alarmed. During their next lunch meeting, Millie brought more news from the church compound.

"They bought the accident scene. The burned license plate led the county sheriff to the church. Reverend Royce identified Hans as the driver. The Sheriff has scheduled an autopsy in three days.

"There is one other bit of news. I don't know if it means anything to you or not. Betty introduced me to a new arrival, whom she introduced as just plain Richard.

The minute he opened his mouth I knew he was a German."

"Good, tell me anything you find out about this Richard. Also watch how Hubert acts around 'just plain Richard.' That might tell us a lot." El didn't explain what prompted her interest. *Could it be him?*

The Nazi leadership sent another ex-Nazi, Richard Baer, Werner's former commander, to be the new organizer for the American Reich. Richard Baer, the last Camp Commander at Auschwitz, had slipped through the Allies' war-criminals net. Baer was a priority target for the DIN and of special interest to El.

Reverend Royce's church had no problem harboring fugitives who were like-minded about racial and religious purity. Already the church compound held a past Grand Dragon of the Texas Ku Klux Klan.

When Millie shared that Hubert appeared to be guarding Richard, El sent a request for a copy of any photo of Richard Baer that the DIN might possess. It took three weeks for the only known picture of the Nazi to reach her. El showed Millie the picture of Richard Baer resplendent in his SS uniform. When Millie said, "That looks like him," El shivered in anticipation.

Richard Baer had come to north Idaho as the replacement for dead doctor Kleinheintz. He would oversee the indoctrination and training of a new generation of *Werwolfs*. What Herr Baer found upon arrival in Hayden Lake was two dead Nazis. Accidents perhaps, but then even paranoids have real fears.

Is there an informant among us at the Purity Church compound? This he had to know before he could rebuild the Reich. Baer shared his suspicion with the reverend and with Hubert. Baer's concern remained a closely held secret since an informant could be among the church inner circle or its growing congregation. Their hunt was on.

21. Johnny, 1952

Unknown to the Nazis, concerns about the Aryans had already begun. The church had hit the radar of the Kootenai County Sheriff. Then the FBI entered the picture when they identified the former Grand Dragon of the Texas Ku Klux Klan, wanted on federal charges, secluded in the church compound.

Shared interest makes for strange bed fellows. The lone FBI Agent in Coeur d' Alene, Steve Jurnigan, needed an informant inside the church compound.

A Coeur d' Alene local, Johnny Palmieri, had a pending federal case. The FBI offered Johnny a chance to work off his case by going undercover. Anything that kept him out of federal prison was fine with Johnny. By first attending church services and spouting racist and anti-Semitic bullshit, Johnny had been welcomed into the reverend's fold in 1952, before either of the Nazis had their accidents.

Over time, Johnny attracted the attention of Reverend Royce and Commandant Baer. He was too vocal and almost a caricature of what racial purity actual meant. Too loud, too fervent and too boastful, Palmieri could be the informant and had to be eliminated.

With Richard Baer in the compound, Hubert's attention was now focused on guarding his former camp commander, so the reverend needed a new Chief of Security. Elmer Crookshank, a retired sheriff's deputy, stepped up to the job.

At the top of Elmer's list was identifying the informant that Reverend Royce and Richard Baer believed was hiding within their midst. Elmer also suspected Johnny Palmieri. Palmieri was too enthusiastic in his racist and anti-Semitic diatribes. He was too eager, trying too hard to be everything that would impress the reverend. His arrival, just before the losses of Werner and Hans, also seemed too coincidental.

Reverend Royce and Elmer shared their concerns with the church's inner circle. They decided Palmieri needed to take a long dirt nap. Elmer's suggestion was to hire out the job of removing Johnny. The fewer links between the church and Johnny's disappearance the better.

Elmer knew where to find and how to recognize the local criminal underworld. He knew that once he floated his offer, word would get around, but he had to be patient.

* * * *

Stanley Romano hated north Idaho. He craved the excitement of a big city. Drinking, fighting and fornicating were at the top of his testosterone- and adrenalin-filled wish list. Washing dishes in a quiet, sparsely settled resort town was nowhere in the catalog. As soon as the giant Brizzalera loosened his control, Stanley began scheming.

He got his first adrenalin fix in Coeur d' Alene. Walking through an alley behind Sherman Avenue, he happened upon a strong-arm robbery in progress. Two men were beating a skinny, middle-aged fella. They had their victim on the ground. Their punches had progressed to kicks. All Stanley saw was an invitation to fight, and he happily entered the fray. When the two attackers fled, Stanley helped the victim up off the asphalt and handed him his broken glasses.

The grateful man rewarded his young savior by providing him alcohol on request. Better yet, 'Bob the Victim' provided information. Bob worked for the Coeur d' Alene newspaper's circulation department. It was Bob whom subscribers called to arrange a 'stop delivery' when they went on vacation.

With Stanley's mornings free, 'Bob the Victim', completed the trifecta of crime: opportunity, alcohol and inside information. Lacking a vehicle, Stanley could only take small things: cash, jewelry and handguns. It was the alcohol, too early and too much, that tripped him up.

Visibly intoxicated as he walked away from a successful burglary, Stanley drew the attention of a random patrol. The police knew about the rise in daytime residential burglaries. Staggering Stanley was stopped. When he failed 'the attitude test,' Stanley found himself in handcuffs. A curbside pat-down for weapons discovered a pistol in the waistband of his trousers and pockets full of cash and jewelry.

* * * *

Agent Jurnigan got word from his on-the-street informants that Palmieri was marked for death. The Aryans were shopping around for a hitman. Palmieri had to be extracted, permanently and soon. Jurnigan was told to recruit locally for the bit-part of hitman for hire.

He first looked for a hitter who wanted to work off a sentence. None appeared. Next Jurnigan, an ex-Marine himself, began looking at veterans living in Idaho. He found two good candidates: Frank Gagliardi, the former Marine Raider, and Vernon Dawson, a decorated Army vet. Digging deeper the Agent found that Dawson was an African American, so unsuited for the job at hand. Frank, who lived and worked as a cook in Coeur d' Alene, fit the part. Could Gagliardi be bribed with money? Did he have a pending criminal case? What hold could the FBI have on him?

Gagliardi's boss had known mob ties and the Bureau already knew that Spirit Lake, Idaho was where the east coast mob sent their people to cool off. The mob and the Bureau had a long history of back scratches, With Johnny Palmieri's life hanging in the balance, Agent Jurnigan made contact with Frank.

The Agent and the former Marine Raider met in the kitchen at Luigi's restaurant. Lou Brizz, Frank's boss and east coast mob contact, was also at the table. Jurnigan described what he needed, a pretend hit man to fake Palmieri's murder. The idea was to both extract Palmieri and perhaps set up Gagliardi as a go-to killer for hire.

"What's in it for us?" asked Frank.

"What do you want?" responded Agent Jurnigan.

Frank and Brizz excused themselves from the table. When they returned to the conversation, Brizz spoke for them both. "Frank's assistant has a pending case in Coeur d' Alene. If you get his charges dismissed, Frank can help you."

"What's the fella's name and what's the charge?"

"Stanley Romano, burglary, five counts."

"I'll see what I can do and then I'll be back in touch, but my need for you is time dependent. If I can squash the burglary charges, you have to be ready to go."

* * * *

With Agent Jurnigan gone, Frank and Brizz sat silently at the table.

"Lou, you're the boss, no question. I've got to tell you that this whole situation scares me, and not many things can do that."

Brizz raised his gaze from the tabletop to Frank's face. The giant only gave a slight nod, acknowledging his understanding that Frank Gagliardi had been afraid of nothing, so the words just spoken were not voiced easily.

"I still see dead Japs in my sleep. Seeing the women and kids is the hardest. But I live with the visits. It was kill or be killed back on those islands."

Brizz lowered his gaze back to the tabletop. "Sometimes I hear the screams of the wounded; ours—theirs, the screams were all the same."

"Listen, the Nazis don't scare me. Jurnigan and what he wants doesn't scare me. Here's the thing, for the first time in my life I've found someone who understands my demons."

"Because she has demons of her own?"

"She does. She's still dealing with hers, but somehow both our demons stay away when we're together."

"This is Millie's friend?"

Franks gave a silent confirmation by cutting his eyes from Brizz to the tabletop and back to his boss. "I think she's maybe my last chance."

"I've seen her wrist. The six numbers. Do her demons start there?"

"Yes."

"Are there more demons up on the rim rock?"

"Yes."

The giant grunted but didn't speak.

"Listen Brizz, I'd be either in a cell or dead if it wasn't for Primo Lagomarsino." Frank paused, "and for you. You and this place, this kitchen, they saved my life. I'll do whatever the family needs, no questions. I should have kept a better eye on the kid. But, it scares the shit out of me when I think about killing. Just so you know."

Brizz shifted his bulk in the chair; his massive shoulders rolled, and he cracked his knuckles before speaking.

"Stanley is a triple asshole. I can't say more now, but he's on his way out. Let's leave it at that for the moment. I'll tell Jurnigan that we have a deal."

* * * *

In the Kootenai County jail, Stanley's cellmate, Bruce, was awaiting trial for passing Aryan-made counterfeit money. Young Stanley was a captive audience as Bruce railed against all of his persecutors, both real and imagined. Stanley shared the unfairness of his own situation. He'd finally got what he wanted. A booze connection, a steady lay from his boss's wife, and a thriving criminal side business.

Bruce had successfully passed Aryan counterfeit money for the better part of the previous year. The counterfeiting operation ran out of the church compound where the phony $20 bills were produced. The newly made money was aged by wrinkling and tumbling it in a clothes dryer. Then as a last touch the bills were given a brief tea bath.

All had gone well with this money-making scheme. The $20 bills were of a small enough denomination that they garnered little attention from clerks. The beginning of the end came when the operation, flush with success but impatient to raise more money for the 'whites only' homeland, switched from twenties to fifties. The bigger bills got more scrutiny, and the public wised up. When merchants took in bad bills, it was their loss. Crowds of victims were screaming for blood, and the government responded by establishing a Secret Service task force, which soon nabbed Bruce.

Stanley listened to his older cellmate. He could relate to Bruce's claims of victimhood, because he also thought of himself as a victim. The two bonded over shared beliefs of their own entitlement and victimhood. To Stanley, the call to action preached by Bruce was a siren song.

"I'm telling you, you can't trust the government. They are in bed with the Jews. Could I find a job? No! All the jobs are taken by the mud people. The feds would rather give a boost to the coons and the spiks than give white Americans an even break."

* * * *

The Kootenai County jail in Coeur d' Alene was both small and old. Visits were supervised by a disinterested deputy sitting in the corner of the visiting room.

When Brizz arrived, Stanley was already sitting at one of the three small round tables in the room. The sleeves of his orange jumpsuit were folded up, putting his muscles on display. The giant went to slide his chair back from the table but couldn't. The table and chairs were bolted to the cement floor, a previously hard-learned lesson about keeping furniture from being weaponized.

"You all right?"

"Nobody fucks with me in here." Rolling his shoulders and subtly flexing his muscles, the young killer tried to communicate invincibility. Brizz watched the young tough's preening. Leaning forward Brizz delivered the first of two messages.

"Frank and I are working on fixing this situation with the burglaries. Try not to cause us any more trouble while you're here."

"Yah, I know. Next time I'll be more careful and lay off the booze."

"What have you got, shit for brains? You're here because you screwed up bad before."

Stanley stared across the table but made no response to the big man. It was time for Brizz to deliver his second, more personal message.

"No girls in here. That makes it tough." Stanley had slouched back in his chair, but at the mention of girls he leaned in, his forearms now resting on the table.

"So, what kind of girls do you like? Do you like the ones with the big butts? The kind that go '*boom-dela-boom-dela-boom*" when they walk?"

Stanley smirked a "No."

"How about the ones with the big tits? The ones that go, "*gigida-gigida-gigida*" and Brizz put his palms up chest high, gently alternating hand motions pantomiming bouncing breasts. "That what you like?"

"Not so much, I like the high hard ones."

157

"Aha," said Brizz with a knowing smile.

"The big girls that are all soft and round, like with the big arms that wave "wappita-wappita-wappita" when they move." Brizz smiled as he rhythmically swayed his wrist and elbow to imitate the flap of skin hanging from fat arms.

"No, I don't like that so much either." Concern or confusion began creeping into the young hoodlum's voice as the giant Brizz leaned closer, his face now only inches away.

"So, if you don't like those things, why are you fuckin' my wife?" One large hand descended onto the orange shoulder and thick fingers squeezed for a single painful moment. Brizz released his grip before the deputy looked up from his magazine.

"I'll have your shit delivered to the jail. You're on your own now. Our family can understand the burglaries. That's stealing from somebody else. But two things we don't do are steal from the family or screw another family member's wife."

* * * *

Finding himself homeless, Stanley turned to his cellmate, Bruce. Feeling more victimized than ever, Stanley added to his list of "Who's to Blame for My Problems" the very man who'd offered him a home, job and new start.

"The big bastard cut me loose. It's not my fault that his fat old lady wanted some of me. Anyway, fuck em."

Bruce listened in silence, which Stanley took as sympathy and agreement.

"So, can I come up to the rim rock with your people up there?"

Seeing a potential use for the violence-loving young thug, Bruce was happy to extend a welcome on behalf of the Aryans. Stanley moved into the Purity Church compound on the day of their release from jail.

22. The Abduction, 1953

Frank's act was ready to begin when he received the expected heads up from Agent Jurnigan.

Pretending to be a hit man for hire, he made a call to the church and asked for Elmer. He arranged a sit-down meeting at a seedy bar in Coeur d' Alene. Amid the smells of cigarettes and spilled beer Elmer laid a picture of Johnny Palmieri on the tabletop in the dimly lit corner of the bar.

"Here is his schedule at the compound, where he lives and what he drives. We want him to disappear with no connection to the church."

"When?"

"Soonest."

"$5,000," said the quiet killer. "Half up front and the balance upon proof the job's done. Call this number when you decide." The faux hit man walked away from the table.

Elmer took the offer back to the church's inner circle. They quibbled about the price but finally agreed.

"Can we slip in some of our counterfeit?" wondered one of the leaders.

"Don't be stupid. I will not be the guy who tries to cheat a professional killer. That idea is all kinds of bad. We pay him and we never see him again," admonished Elmer.

The Elders adjourned to debate, and one hour later Elmer was told he'd have the money tomorrow.

A second meeting was arranged once the cash was in hand. As a precaution, Hubert accompanied Elmer to the rendezvous in the parking lot of the same Coeur d' Alene bar. As the envelope changed hands, Frank said, "I will bring you a picture of his severed head. The number you called gets disconnected tomorrow. When the job is done, I'll put a classified ad in the local paper. When you see, 'Liquidation Sale,' with a date, time and place, I get my money and you your proof."

"How long will this take, do you think?" asked Crookshank.

"One week," was the response.

* * * *

Jurnigan picked the place for Johnny Palmieri's extraction five days hence. The disappearance had to look like a kidnapping, or the Aryans might know they'd been duped. The plan was for his car to be found abandoned at a rest stop between Hayden Lake and Coeur d' Alene. The editor of the Coeur d' Alene Press was recruited to ensure a page one story and picture about the apparent kidnapping. Elmer and his bosses would be led down the path of misinformation.

Next, Jurnigan set about creating the proof of death the Aryans expected. He brought a bureau photographer to town, along with a retired Hollywood make-up artist. A Spokane warehouse became an improvised photographic studio.

Palmieri sat flat on the cement floor under a car. His head protruded through a hole cut in the floor of the trunk. A carefully slit blanket went over his head and across the bottom of the trunk. Then the make-up artist created the gore and pallor needed to fool the Aryans. The tableau, Palmeri's severed head in the hitman's trunk, was photographed with a Polaroid Instamatic camera provided by the bureau. With the gas tank reinstalled and the trunk repaired, the appearance of Frank's car trunk supported the ruse.

With the job completed, the "Liquidation Sale" notice appeared in the classified section of the local paper. Then Jurnigan told Johnny about the future.

"Mr. Palmieri, your case will be dismissed later today. I'm informing the Assistant United States Attorney of your considerable help. Because the Aryans think you're dead, they need to keep that idea, so you are getting a new name and a new home." Jurnigan handed Johnny a manila folder containing a one-page biography.

'John Boccolini' read the bold heading at the top of the page. Boccolini lived and worked in Fort Smith, Arkansas. Paper-clipped to the biography sheet were a bus ticket and $2,000 in $100 bills.

"For your own continued good health, I suggest you never come back to Idaho. Thanks for your help. I'll drive you to the bus depot in Spokane."

"When?"

"Now."

* * * *

Elmer and Hubert arrived at the appointed time and place. Frank Gagliardi was waiting. Jurnigan and two agents from the Spokane field office monitored the meet. They photographed the pay-off in anticipation of a future trial.

Frank handed the Polaroids of Palmieri's severed head to Elmer and Hubert. For added credibility, the bloodstained blanket in the picture was still in Frank's trunk. There was a long pause as the two caucused. "Where's the body now?" asked Elmer.

"Burned."

Again, the two conferred. Frank leaned against his car and fired up a cigarette. His bare arms displayed the Marine 'globe and anchor' on one side. The 'Skull' unit patch image of his Marine Raiders was tattooed on the other.

It was Curtis who handed over the second $2500 fee. "Good job. We might have need of your services again. How can I get in touch?"

"You got a pencil?"

Crookshank produced a pen. Frank dropped his cigarette and crushed the butt with his shoe, wrote a number inside a match book and passed it back.

The exchange of 'proof' for cash took five minutes. The Aryans returned to their compound. Frank drove to a prearranged meeting site in Coeur d' Alene. There he handed over the $2500 to Agent Jurnigan.

"Stanley's case will be dismissed with prejudice this afternoon, as promised."

"If Crookshank calls, I'll let you know." Frank lit a cigarette with his bronze Zippo.

23. Changing Tribes, 1953

Cellmates Bruce and Stanley both gained their release on the same day. Stanley's case was dismissed because, according to his court-appointed attorney, the evidence had been misplaced and was not available for trial.

Bruce didn't have a discoverable prior criminal record. After giving profound, heartfelt apologies to his victims and to the court, he received a suspended sentence and two years' unsupervised probation.

* * * *

"If you turn out to be as solid as I think you are, you could be an Aryan warrior, like me. And if you show me you've got balls and are trustworthy, ask me to tell you about the Kike I killed in Denver."

Stanley looked like a potential recruit into the Aryan's branch of God's army. He had all the qualities The Order valued: no scruples, no future, a love of violence, and an obsequious desire to be led. He was a willing follower of anyone who cultivated his self-image as a victim.

The Aryans had learned valuable lessons about informants. Stanley would be introduced to their movement in slow stages. First, he'd march in the upcoming White Pride parade through downtown Coeur d' Alene. If he publicly wore the Storm Trooper uniform and carried the red, white and black Swastika flag, it would validate his loyalty.

Stanley marched in the church's first-ever White Pride parade down Sherman Avenue. He held the Swastika flag above his head and wore a Swastika armband. The parade was well covered by the local newspapers. Wire service photographers snapped pictures that appeared on many a front page all across the country. Stanley the young, strong, and proud flag bearer enjoyed his own moment of fame in thousands of newsprint pictures.

* * * *

Primo was sipping his breakfast coffee when he saw the pictures from north Idaho. His interest turned to anger when he recognized Stanley Romano. Primo, like his friend Brizz, was a World War I veteran. As a proud Italian American living on the heels of another world war where Italy had been an enemy, he had little sympathy for any belief system that venerated Nazis. The message came directly to Brizz from Primo's lips. "End this."

* * * *

"Did you get the word from Brizz? He wants us at the restaurant, tonight at ten P.M. for a meeting."

"I did," replied Duano in response to Frank's question. Monday night, with the restaurant closed, was the best time for meetings.

Frank joined Brizz at the table in the kitchen corner. The big man had retrieved a bottle of grappino and three glasses from the bar. The first drink was not poured until Duano arrived and seated himself.

"Primo called. The pictures of Stanley in his Storm Trooper uniform and carrying their 'crooked cross' flag were in all the east coast papers. He's starting to get shit from the other families. Stanley is embarrassing our family. His exact words were, 'Make this shit stop.'"

Two sets of eyes switched from Brizz to their glasses. Duano took his first sip. Frank rolled the clear liquid around in his glass. Brizz swallowed his shot in one long sip. The three knew that they were not here to deliberate Stanley's fate. As soldiers in the same army, they never questioned an order from above. Theirs was only to decide the best way to carry out Primo's order.

Duano spoke first. "I'll do it."

"No, I'll do it. The kid worked for me and I can get close to him." Frank's voice cut the silence as he too looked to the giant.

"No, it's my responsibility," said Brizz.

"We're all involved, but the duty is mine, because Primo entrusted him to me. Duano, can you get a message through your wife to their compound?"

Duano nodded. "I'll make sure it happens. What do you want him to be told?"

"Tell him Frank needs his help with something, out at the Spirit Lake resort. He knows where."

"When do you want him there?" Duano asked Brizz.

"Tell the kid Wednesday at six P.M. That gives you two days to get the word to him."

Frank and Duano signaled their understanding.

"Frank and I will meet the kid. I'll take it from there." Nothing more was said. No further explanation was needed. The three men all knew how the Wednesday meeting would end.

* * * *

The message passed from Duano to Millie, and on to Bonnie. Confirmation of delivery reached Millie the next morning and Duano that same evening.

"I need to run into Coeur d' Alene. I'll be back in a couple hours." If Millie wondered why her husband had to make the trip, she said nothing. Rosie needed her after-dinner bath.

"Drive careful. I love you."

Duano entered through the kitchen door at Luigi's. Frank was busy at the eight-burner stove. A prep-cook worked on assembling a pasta dish at the 'pass' as a waiter stood by. A woman assembled salads and a rubber-aproned dishwasher busied himself scraping plates at sinks in the far back.

Duano waited until Frank turned around to plate the scaloppini dish he'd completed. When their eyes met, Duano gave a slow nod. Frank acknowledged with a nod, and Duano left through the back door. The meeting was on. Frank told Brizz after the last of the employees had departed.

* * * *

Stanley Romano didn't question his former boss's request, but lacking a car, he needed a ride to the Shady Rest Resort. The reverend provided both car and driver. When the two drove under the entry arch, Stanley began looking for Frank, who waved him down when the car passed the last cabin on the lakeshore.

"Tell your friend we'll give you a lift home when we're done."

Stanley did as he was told.

"Brizz needs to see you. He's inside the cabin."

Stanley was nervous after the discovery of his adultery, but he followed Frank inside. Brizz sat at the wooden table and motioned for Stanley to take a seat. Frank brought him a beer and clicked his own long-neck bottle against Stanley's in a toast.

Brizz waited, allowing Stanley to down half his bottle before he began. "Why the Nazi shit?"

Draining his beer, Stanley began parroting all the biblical excuses that he'd retained in his head. Another beer appeared by his side.

"Do you believe that shit about 'mud people, the blacks and the Jews'?"

Stanley, nervous at being challenged, responded by sucking down more beer. "Yeah, everybody knows about the Jews controlling the government. We know about their plan to weaken our Aryan race by allowing race mixing." He finished his second beer. Frank set down a third bottle. He and Brizz shook their heads in response to the torrent of mindless, baseless bullshit.

The three men stayed silent as Frank handed Brizz his first beer. There was nothing more to be said, so they drank their beers in silence.

"I need to piss," announced Stanley. Frank pointed to the one interior door. When Stanley got up, it was time. Frank stood opposite the bathroom door. Brizz moved to a spot that hid him when the door opened. They both heard the flush. When the victim came out, Frank was standing at the table, but no Brizz.

"Where'd he go?"

"He went outside to piss." Those were the last words Stanley heard as the giant dropped the piano-wire garrote over his head and began a controlled pull on the wooden end pieces. Frank grabbed the victim's kicking legs, and Brizz continued the gradual strangulation, careful to not decapitate Stanley. When all motion ceased, Brizz removed the garrote, and the lifeless body rested at his feet.

Brizz carried the body under one enormous arm and placed it gently in the boat. Frank met him at the waters' edge and added a cinder block and the garrote-wire necklace to the cargo. The mob had long known about and used the same sink hole that El favored. The skiff was too small for them both, so Frank rowed out into the lake alone. From the beach, Brizz surveyed the surrounding shores for onlookers. No one around, he signaled to Frank. Stanley slipped over the side to his last rest.

Duano got a confirmation call from Frank and he knew what message to pass on through Millie.

"Tell them, Stanley stopped by after the lake meeting and told me he had second ts about being involved with the church. Frank put him on a bus back east. Would you let the folks on the rim rock know?"

24. Betrayal

The ideologies of the Aryans and the Nazis significantly overlapped but sprang from different poisoned roots. The Nazis worked for the Fourth Reich with all of its hateful goals. The Aryans wanted a separatist, whites-only homeland and an absolute end to interracial marriage.

As El planned revenge on the Nazis, she was aware of the separate evil of Reverend Royce's church. Only one of the two evils was her focus and concern, except where they overlapped.

She held former Auschwitz Commandant Richard Baer and former guard Hubert Schwarz responsible for the deaths of her family. It didn't lessen either's guilt that they were 'only following orders,' as numerous Nuremberg defendants had claimed.

With Baer and his guard, Hubert, now operating almost as one, her task became more difficult. A single event could punish them both, but crafting her action was now more complicated. Baer found the church compound a useful base of operations for his primary task, building his *Werwolfs* and resurrecting the Reich. The Aryans were useful but dull tools in pursuit of the future Nazi empire.

El considered multiple plans for isolating Baer and Schwarz. Then her focus abruptly shifted. Could she get the Nazis to do the job for her? El shared her ideas with Millie as they lunched. Ultimately, it was Millie who sparked El to her best option.

Her idea was to use a letter as a weapon. Polishing the idea, El settled on the story line she'd plant among the Nazis. She'd need Millie's help to sell the narrative. El would write the letter, and Millie would arrange its discovery.

> Darling Richard,
> The days are so long without you. The life you've given me is wonderful. I've never enjoyed such luxury as you provide. The spa, the maid, the Mercedes are so expensive. While I love them, I love you more. I worry that your organization might discover the money you are spending on me. I am still the simple girl who fell in love with you so many years ago. Still my days are empty without you.
> When everyone else saw me only as a dirty Jew, you saw me as a person. I loved you with all my heart from the moment we met. Beyond all things, thank you for ridding me of that pig Werner. I couldn't have lived another day tolerating his embrace. The wounds he inflicted on my body are starting to heal, thanks to you. We have stolen enough money to last all our days. Come to me, my love.
> Your loving Rachael.

Millie read over the letter El had crafted. The single first-class stamp also fit the idea of a local mistress.

"You're good. When I get this into Hubert's hands, Richard will have to explain stealing from the Nazis, killing his predecessor, and keeping a Jewish mistress."

"We'll get one shit bag to kill another shit bag for us," El responded.

"Just keep the letter someplace safe and find it on the floor of the store after Baer comes in. Then give the note to Bonnie. She'll give it to her husband, and he'll pass it to Hubert."

* * * *

If successful, El's plan would set in motion a series of actions, all without her direct involvement. It took a week for Richard Baer to visit the Bayview store. Since Reverend Royce's wife was the proprietress, the Nazis and the church staff considered it a safe haven. Richard Baer came for tobacco and got more than he'd bargained for. Twenty-minutes later the trap was sprung.

"Bonnie, I found this letter on the floor by our counter. I think maybe Mr. Baer dropped it." And Millie handed over the faux love note.

"It's already been opened, so I'll sneak a peek," responded Bonnie. What she read momentarily stopped her breathing. Bonnie read it again, and her concern doubled. She refolded the note and returned it to the envelope.

"Was it Mr. Baer's?"

Bonnie didn't reply. Instead she told Millie she'd be out of the store for a while and left. Millie knew the sequence of events she'd set in motion.

* * * *

Arriving at the compound gate, Bonnie laid her hand on the car horn. Once, twice, three times she honked. She needed entry now! Hearing the horn blasts, her husband came out of the church office. Then Curtis stuck his head out from the print shop. When the horn sounded again, both Royce and Curtis descended on the gate.

Bonnie gestured to the men as they opened the gate. She handed the letter to her husband through the car window. "Read this and say nothing to anybody." As she parked next to the church office, the reverend read the note and then passed it to Curtis.

"Let's go into my office." Curtis and Bonnie followed.

Their closed-door meeting took 30 minutes. They all saw the three betrayals that the letter suggested. Digesting the note's implication, the reverend summoned his Chief of Security. Elmer Crookshank read the note in silence and then got the explanation of how, when and where it had been found. Only then did he speak.

"We killed the wrong man. Palmieri was a fool, but he had no part in Kleinheintz's death." The four voices continued in a worried discussion of how to proceed.

"We have to show Hubert the letter. While Baer is a Jew-loving thief, he is stealing from them and it was one of them he killed," Curtis summarized.

"I say we let the Nazis deal with him," voiced the reverend. Three heads nodded in agreement.

"Elmer, can you get Hubert away from Baer?"

"I can tell Baer that you need to speak to him. While you two are behind closed doors, I'll talk to Hubert. He'll know how they want to handle this." While the reverend distracted Baer, Elmer briefed Hubert and handed over the found note.

"*Mein Gott!*" the former Auschwitz guard whispered after reading the faux love letter. "I will contact our leadership for instructions. We know how to make pigs squeal. We just twist their tails. Thank you. I will let you know what we decide."

Hubert Schwarz made phone contact with an unknown person somewhere on the east coast. He read the letter aloud to the voice on the other end of the line. Next he described how the note had come into his possession. The circumstances and content El and Millie had created all hung together and vouched for the note's authenticity.

"Call back tomorrow, Herr Schwarz, and I will have instructions for you," and the voice was gone.

* * * *

Later that afternoon, when Bonnie returned to her store in Bayview, Millie asked about the letter.

"It was just a note from Richard Baer's wife telling him his oldest daughter got engaged."

As Millie listened, she heard the worry in her boss's voice. "Are you OK?"

The content of the letter had profoundly upset everyone 'in the know,' and Bonnie was having a hard time concealing the agitation. "No, it's nothing," she protested. Next she switched her tone, hoping that a mild rebuke would fend off Millie's curiosity.

"If you must know, I'm uncomfortable having read someone else's mail. You should know that nice people just don't do that."

Aware of the real content of the note, Millie interpreted Bonnie's lies and deflections as proof they had swallowed the bait. She'd share the news with El tomorrow at lunch.

* * * *

The following day Hubert Schwarz arranged to be alone so he could check back as he'd been instructed.

"Herr Schwarz, we are concerned. I think you know how to do a proper interrogation."

"How vigorous am I to be?"

"I authorize you to use any methods to get the truth."

"And then?"

"And then eliminate the traitor," directed the voice, and the line clicked off, leaving only a busy signal.

Hubert Schwarz informed Security Chief Crookshank of his orders from above.

"What you do is your business. Where you do it is my business. Use the storage shed out at our rifle range for your interrogation. Then, if Baer is terminated, his body won't be on church grounds. I will arrange disposal. Understood?"

Hubert understood Crookshank fine.

* * * *

Richard Baer was easily lured out to the rifle range. He'd not committed any of the crimes El's fake love note suggested, so he was completely unsuspecting. The range storage shed held supplies. Paper targets, coffee cans for shell casings, spotting scopes and sandbags lined its walls. Baer entered the shed as Hubert switched on the overhead light. A wooden chair sat in the middle of the room.

Hubert slipped his hands into thin leather gloves as he spoke. "Herr Baer."

Richard turned.

Hubert found it effective to administer an initial beating before asking his first question. The pain communicated both his seriousness and willingness to use violence. Bruised and bloodied, Baer was pushed down into the chair. The former guard had learned that his silence, coupled with the interviewee's imagination, was more terrible than anything he could show or say, so he waited.

"I will ask you questions. If you tell me the truth, the pain stops. If you lie, the beating resumes. Do you understand?"

Through bloody lips, Baer squealed, "But I've done nothing."

"We know what you have done, Herr Baer. We only want to hear you acknowledge your guilt." With that, Hubert struck another blow.

"Now we start again. Where is the money you have stolen from us?" On it went, Hubert asking a question and Richard pleading ignorance. Another beating followed, but still no confession.

"Why did you kill Herr Kleinheintz?" Again, Baer whimpered a denial and then came another beating. Richard, having nothing to confess, could only plead and endure. Hubert's voice was never loud. His control hinted at an underlying reasonableness to listen and to believe the cries of, "I'm innocent, I'm innocent."

"Where is your Jew mistress, Herr Baer?"

Now the answers came through broken teeth as blood and saliva dribbled down his chin. "I have no mistress. I'm loyal to the Reich."

The questioning ended when Hubert decided that there was nothing more to be gained. The unconscious Baer slumped in the wooden chair. There was no need for conferring with his superiors, but he would report his findings anyway. Now he'd secure Baer while he called and arranged disposal.

From long experience Hubert had his favorite means of control. Baer would stay in the unheated shed for now. Schwarz picked up a hammer and two ten-penny nails already inside the shed. Hubert pulled down the unconscious man's trousers and underwear. He drove first one and then a second nail through Baer's scrotum into the seat of the wooden chair.

* * * *

Hubert Schwarz made his report to the voice on the other end of the phone. A long pause ensued.

"Liquidate him" was the instruction.

Hubert understood what needed to be done. The body was not to be buried on church property. He could leave Baer's corpse in the woods for the animals, but his bones would be discernably human. So, Schwarz turned to Elmer Crookshank.

Elmer wanted nothing to connect the church with Baer's disappearance or his body, if it were ever found. He turned to his go-to hired killer, Frank Gagliardi.

That afternoon Elmer sat in a back booth in the same seedy Coeur d' Alene bar where he'd first met Frank.

At the appointed hour Frank arrived. Grabbing a draft beer at the bar, he joined Elmer in the booth. Unlike their first meeting, the FBI was not involved. His relationship with El and all it implied had changed his focus from helping the feds to helping the woman he loved. He drank his beer in silence as he waited for Elmer to make the first move.

Checking that no one was there to overhear the conversation, he began. "I've got another job, if you are interested."

Frank said nothing as he studied the bubbles in his beer.

"It's a disposal."

"Alive or dead?"

Elmer held Frank in his gaze. "Yeah, one or the other. Is that a problem?"

"Nope, I'm charging the same either way. Is that a problem for you?"

Elmer shook his head.

"Pictures?" asked Frank.

"No, just disposal."

"Last question. Is this a local who's likely to be missed?"

Elmer stayed silent. When Frank held him in a steady stare, he knew an answer was needed. "No, it's a kraut."

With the price agreed, the two arranged for Frank to pick up 'the garbage'. It would be just off the roadside at a spot along the church compound's fence. Frank would be looking for a dirty sleeping bag. The pickup would be that night.

* * * *

Frank made one call immediately after leaving the bar.

"Hey, it's me. I've got something. The assholes up on the rim rock hired me to dispose of some garbage. The garbage is a kraut. Interested in seeing who I'm getting?"

"Yes," was El's response.

He arranged to meet her at the Shady Rest Resort in Spirit Lake. "If it's who you were hoping to find, can he be your last? Please."

"I can't answer, because I won't lie to you, ever. I'll never kill again for money. But some of the demons are still here and they owe me a personal debt."

* * * *

Hubert was waiting for Crookshank back at the church compound. The two men went to the rifle range shed. Richard was now awake and pleading for his life, again to no avail. When dark overcame the day, Hubert knocked Baer out, taped his mouth shut and bound his wrists and ankles. He cut the heads off the nails that held Baer to the chair.

Baer's unconscious body was then put in a sleeping bag. The men carried the bag to the fence that surrounded the main compound. They dumped Baer over the top strand of barbed wire. Richard had become just another piece of roadside trash.

Twenty minutes later the bag went into Frank's car trunk for the twelve-mile drive to Spirit Lake. Frank knew the owners of the resort. He'd called ahead to arrange access to one of the resort's aluminum boats and their most remote cabin.

Frank arrived first and checked the bag for signs of life. The bag twitched and moaned when he poked it. He reclosed the trunk lid.

When El stepped out of her car, intensity was evident in her stride and unblinking glare. Frank opened the trunk and partially unzipped the sleeping bag. Bruised and bloodied, Richard Baer struggled to focus his eyes.

179

As El stared at the face in the bag, Frank clicked on his flashlight. Baer, still gagged, moaned and tried to turn his head as the beam shocked his dilated pupils.

El searched her memory for the face in the beam, and there it was. Overwhelmed by memories of Auschwitz, she remembered her last view of her family. They were sorted, some to live, others to die, on the day of their arrival. Involuntary tears filled her eyes. Turning back to the face in the bag, first El delivered a hard slap. Then she spat on Richard Baer.

With her right hand she gripped his cheeks, forcing him to look directly at her. Frank angled the flashlight beam out of Baer's eyes and onto his lover's left forearm when El held it up. There was the six-digit number tattooed, stark black against her white skin. Baer's eyes widened as he recognized the Auschwitz tattoo. She silently held this monster in her glare while Baer attempted to avert his gaze.

"Commandant Baer, look who is killing you: a Jewess. You die tonight, but I give you one choice that you never gave any of your victims. You can die hard or die easy," and El paused, her gaze never wavering.

"If you tell me where I can find another Nazi, you earn an easy death." And then she slammed the trunk lid shut.

Frank turned off his flashlight and the two figures standing alone in the dark found the comfort of each other's arms. He stroked her back as it vibrated from the rise and fall of her sobbing chest. Frank kept silent, as no words seemed to fit. Finally, El relaxed her hands from their blood-draining clench and raised her face to his.

"What do you want to do?"

"I want to skin him alive." Her response came in a whisper. "But we don't have time." Drying her eyes on a sleeve El added, "If he gives me a name..." but the sentence hung unfinished.

Frank looked at her face in the moonlight, "If?"

She refocused on the car trunk. "It doesn't matter. He dies the same" and shifting back to regard him, she finished. "I lied. Open the trunk."

As the lid rose, Baer shifted his head to face his killer, and she removed the tape from his mouth.

"Well?"

Panic now in his voice, Baer began to plead for the promised easy death. "Hubert Schwarz, one of my former guards, is at the compound. That's all I know, please believe me."

"And who else?"

"No one else. I don't know where the other cells are. I'm told only when he thinks I need to know something."

"Who tells you?"

"Barbee."

"Klaus Barbee, the butcher of Lyon?"

"Yes."

"Tell me where Barbee can be found, and I'll let you live."

"Please, I don't know where any of them are. They call me."

El made no response to the Nazi. Holding him in her gaze she spoke to Frank. "Take him out of the trunk." As Frank took the top of the bag, she lifted Baer's feet using the bag as handles. "He goes into the boat."

After dumping Baer from the bag into the boat, she forced the tape gag back over his mouth. Frank already knew what to do next. Two cinder blocks were fastened with wire loops to the bound legs. The figure thrashed in panicked protest at the blocks.

"Does the Aryan get a Viking funeral?"

"No, you need a human for that." Then a moment later El added, "But he could be the dog that they placed at the human's feet."

She got into the boat and rowed the short distance out into the mill pond area. The ride ended with the body going into the deepest part of the lake. Richard Baer died like the dog he was.

25.   A Long Shot, September 1953

Ellen Ripley, the dilettante from Bayview, never forgot her true self, Eleanor Greenberg, daughter of Rachael and Shlomo. She had taken Werner, Hans and Richard with her own hands. Only Hubert Schwarz, the former Auschwitz SS guard, remained inside the Purity Church compound. He'd be hers also, but only when she was confident of a plan for his demise.

Having found the first real love of her life in Frank Gagliardi, El could see herself in a life beyond killing if she could drive a stake through the heart of this one final monster. Hubert was a monster, not a fool. As his nest of vipers had been thinned and skinned, his caution had increased. Day after day, she considered and then rejected scenarios. All but one.

El and Millie never stopped their regular lunch meetings. The bond between them that began at the lakeshore had firmed to unbreakable strength when El helped Millie free herself from evil Ed, her blackmailer.

El's perceived debt to Millie was equally strong. It was galvanized by Millie having facilitated the killing of the Auschwitz Commandant and the SS guard. She would help again with any plan that El was considering to kill Hubert Schwarz.

"Does your husband still do the annual elk hunt with Curtis?"

The pregnant Millie looked over the sandwich in her hand and nodded.

"Do the guys ever take anyone else along, or is it just them?"

Millie swigged iced tea to clear her mouth. "I don't know. They don't include wives in their male bonding ritual."

With mutual trust long established, El shared the essence of her idea.

"I'm going to kill Schwarz, the last Nazi at the compound. My plan is to lure him away from his duties and into the woods where I can arrange a hunting accident."

Millie nodded but kept silent.

"If we could get Hubert to join their group, I'd have the opportunity I need. Duano won't be involved in the killing, but he might be encouraged to make an invitation. Here is how we, no actually you, sell it," and El ticked off the key talking points.

"Hold that t, the baby is sitting on my bladder. I'll be right back." She returned minutes later with an answer. "OK, I can try. But my baby's daddy stays in the dark about what's going on. We need to figure a way to make sure that Duano is nowhere around when it happens."

El agreed. "I'll think about it. When do they do this thing? Is hunting season the same time every year?"

"October tenth is the opening and the guys go to camp two days earlier."

"So, let me take a day and see if I can come up with an idea about how to keep Duano away from the fray."

At lunch three days later, El offered her suggestion. "You're due about that time. Suppose you play the pregnancy card?"

"Go on."

"You don't want Duano to miss his annual trip, but it is close to your due date. He needs to have another guy along in case he has to rush home." El paused, letting Millie get comfortable with the unfolding plan.

"Wouldn't it be good to have another person around the campfire? They could use another strong back to help with packing out their elk. I am your back-up in Bayview, and I'll promise to come to hunting camp and get him when your water breaks."

"Ok."

"Duano would need to show me where they have their hunting camp, so I could either find him or find someone there to go look for him or leave a message."

"So then you know where to find Hubert, to track him?"

"Exactly and even better, I can call Duano away if you really do go into labor."

"But what about if I'm not ready and he's still hunting when you go out after the Nazi?"

"If you can tell me what caliber rifle your husband uses, I will use a different common caliber. If the bullet is examined, it won't match Duano's gun. He's still in the clear. Rifle bullets can travel a long way, so the fatal shot could have accidently come from another hunter who doesn't even realize someone got shot. It's just an unfortunate hunting accident."

Millie thought about El's plan. "All right, I'll see if I can sell him on the need for an extra body, at least for this year."

"Don't mention only Hubert. Maybe say Royce or Elmer, and then finally Hubert. It makes his selection seem more random that way."

"But what if one of the others wants to go, or Hubert doesn't or can't?"

"Then you'll just have to get knocked up again," El smiled.

Millie replied with a shocked, "Thanks."

Over the next three weeks, Millie planted the seeds of the plan. She began expressing worry about being alone when her time came.

While Duano was at work, Millie checked the caliber of his rifle, a .300 Winchester Magnum. With that detail now known, El began checking the classified ads. Sure enough, after one week a scoped .270 caliber rifle came up for sale by a private party in Athol. A fatal .270 bullet wound would not implicate Duano.

El also understood that having a rifle with her in the woods during hunting season meant she'd also need a hunting license. No one knew when a random game warden might pull up to their car or camp. The license represented a risk, but so did not having one. To add another layer of separation, El made the license purchase 100 miles from Bayview in Moscow, Idaho.

Living at the edge of town as she did, El's slipping away to practice with the rifle went unnoticed. So did the echoes of her practice shots. This was Idaho after all, and rifle fire, especially in the weeks before elk season, was common. The same anonymity would extend to when she set out on her hunt for Hubert.

"I've played the nervous worry-wart about my delivery. Duano has bought into my suggestion that he bring in an extra hunter this year." Millie went back to sipping her tea between bites of sandwich. "Now we just have to wait and see. I suggested Royce and Elmer, but then I did a worried aftert, 'Oh, but Royce might be too old or Elmer too busy'."

"Let me know what shakes out."

Sold by the guileless fears of a pregnant wife, Duano approached Elmer to join his annual hunt with Curtis. As predicted, Elmer begged off, believing himself to be too busy and too essential to the compound. As hoped, Elmer suggested Hubert Schwarz instead. He'd be a good elk packer and, as an army veteran, was a trained shot. Duano asked Curtis to make the invitation.

"Curtis is someone that Hubert trusts."

When asked, Hubert was flattered. He had always perceived a general reluctance of the Americans to extend themselves personally to their former enemies.

"I need the permission, of the reverend and Security Chief Crookshank, but thank you. I've not been hunting since I went with my father and uncles for years in the Herken Forest. Thank you." He'd taken the bait.

The big German found Curtis at his press after getting the OK from his bosses. With an enthusiastic smile and handshake, Hubert told Curtis he'd join them. Curtis was now an unwitting accomplice. He and Hubert adjourned to the dining hall for coffee. Curtis briefed the German on what he should bring. The list was small, as he and Duano had, over the years, fully equipped their camp.

"All you need is your own sleeping bag, rifle, and a cot if you don't want to sleep on the tent floor. We'll settle up on the food bill later." Then as an aftert Curtis added, "If you don't drink bourbon, bring whatever you want, because Jack Daniel's is all we bring."

One month before opening day, El got the news that her plan was a go. "Ask Duano when he wants to take me out and show me where they camp."

Millie relayed his answer. "He'll take you next Saturday morning, if you're free."

"Tell him fine, I'll be here at 8 A.M. wearing my boots and looking like a mountain princess."

* * * *

Their travel time from Bayview was two hours. The camp was always in the same area. If they were the first hunters on site, a flat spot inside a former rock quarry was their preferred site. If someone beat them to it, three other spots were available within the same area. El noted the milepost next to the hilltop location by what locals called "Bear Wallow."

"OK, if I show up and you're not here, do you have regular spots where you sit or are you walking round?"

"I have a few places where I set up and watch for an animal to walk by. Walking around doesn't work for me. Out here, I'm in the elk's house and he'll hear me before I see him. So, I sit and wait for some animal to walk past. Then I pop him."

"Can you show me your spots, in case I need to find you?"

"You shouldn't be out walking around in the woods during elk season. Some guys see movement and you could get yourself shot. Better just leave a note on our tent flap, if Curtis or Hubert aren't here. They will know where I'll be on any given day, because we don't want to shoot each other by mistake."

El now had what she needed: the camp's location. Even better, she had confirmation that some hunters shot too soon, too far or without a clear picture of their target. Accidents happened, and she'd ensure that one did.

Sunday, the day after her visit to the hunting camp, El returned to the site. The road into the quarry was tree lined. Either side of the turnoff into the quarry offered a discrete vantage point to wait and watch. She'd need to be in her hiding place before sunrise. The forest service road would serve as a safe walking route to her chosen lair, even in the dark. From either side of the access road junction, the campsite would be visible, thirty yards down a gravel path.

With her first problem solved, El stood in the future camp site. Two different trails ran off into the timber. She moved out along one of the old logging roads. Sometimes the roads split into two or more separate trails. Other times they looped back to a connecting point. As she went, a mental picture of the area formed in her mind. Stopping occasionally, she sketched the roads for a mile out from the camp.

Walking the roads, she thought about how she might track Hubert in such a maze of possibilities. She concluded that her plan as conceived was unworkable. At a minimum, either Hubert's route or destination were needed before she set out.

On her way back to town, she checked out options for off-road parking. She finally found a concealed parking spot about 100 yards down the hill from the quarry access point.

* * * *

During their next private lunch meeting, El explained the problem and a possible work-around.

"Ask Duano how Hubert will know where to hunt. He might decide to take the German to one of his own spots rather than having the guy stumbling around in the dark.

You only ask, and we hope he gets the idea and does that."

"But then how do you know where he takes the guy?"

"Duano could take him out ahead of time so he'd know where to go on opening morning. I may be able to follow them out. Worst case, at least I know which road he'll be using. Then I can set up for the next morning on that road. I can follow from a ways back. I keep that up until I've tracked him to his hunting stand."

"Sure, but keep in mind what my husband told you about some hunters shooting at movement in the brush, before they have a clear view. You don't want to be the one getting shot."

El returned to eating her lunch while her mind considered the problem.

"There are some risks I'll just have to take. I'll be as careful as I can, and I may not get my shot. But I won't know until I try, right?"

"All right, there are risks. There were risks with Ed, but it didn't matter to me. I get that risks don't matter to you here. But tell me this; if you shoot the son-of-a-bitch, won't you want to check that he's dead? I mean, would you go up close to look? What if you go to look and he's not dead? Are you going to kill him there and then?"

Stopped by the string of questions, El stared down at her plate.

"I don't know what I'll do if I put him down with one shot but can't tell if he's dead. I'll decide there and then, I guess. If I didn't kill him with my one shot, he still might die of cold or blood loss. At least it will still appear to be a hunting accident and I can try again another day with another plan."

Millie's eyes never wavered from El's face. Her questions were now El's questions and she could only be an outsider to her friend's inner struggles.

"If I go up to his body, I have to kill him and that might cost me the cover of a hunting accident. That would depend on how I finished him off. I'm not sure I'd care, but I won't know that until the decision becomes necessary. So, in the meantime, please plant the suggestion about setting up the Nazi with a particular stand."

It was now two days before the men would leave for camp. Millie fed Duano the line that night at dinner. Between bites of tuna and noodle casserole, Duano mumbled through a partial mouth full, "Good idea. I won't give him my favorite elk rock, but I can put him someplace that will be better than just walking around in the woods."

* * * *

El knew in advance the day when Duano left for camp. She wore every bit of warm clothing she owned plus wool gloves, and topped it all off with a dark blue watch cap. Her pockets were full of jerky, hard candy and a jelly sandwich. A full canteen and a wide-mouthed pee bottle completed her kit. She could not afford to leave any trace of her presence, whether by sight, sound or smell. Her concealed parking spot already selected, El arrived an hour after the three hunters. This was their first of two days setting up and checking old hunting spots for unforeseen changes. As the sun set on their first day at camp, Duano had not taken Hubert out to a hunting spot. El headed home.

She was back in her observation spot the next morning an hour before sunrise. The three men sat around a fire pit. A coffee pot and skillet from their breakfast bacon and eggs sat on the Coleman stove. With their final cups of coffee drained, Duano guided Hubert out of camp. They took the left-hand logging road.

She waited in hiding until Curtis departed down the right-hand road. Skirting the camp, El followed Duano and Hubert's path, being careful to hug the curve of the tree line. As she eased round a wide bend in the trail, the two men appeared up ahead. Stopped in the middle of the road, Duano was pointing to a high bank off to the right. She watched as he led the way off the road up onto the cutbank. Stepping back into the trees, El checked the time. The two men returned to the road five minutes later.

They couldn't have gone far, El t. When the two headed back towards camp, she hunkered down, silent as they passed. Then she went to where they had left the road. She climbed the bank, searching for any clues as to Hubert's likely perch. A collection of boot prints and broken branches showed where the men had stopped. The spot offered two good fields of fire at any animal that came onto the road.

Now she turned her attention to seeking a place from which to make her own shot. El consulted her pencil sketch of the roads and trails network surrounding the quarry. To the experienced huntress, an escape route was of equal importance to her sniper's nest. Each possible shooting position was evaluated for its cover, access to the target, ingress, and egress.

When she'd decided on her spot, El tried different ways of getting in and out. She looked over the availability of cover for her long day or maybe days of watchful waiting. With these issues satisfied, she walked her escape route to within sight of the hunting camp.

El had a choice: stay overnight at her sniper's nest or risk a nightly return to her car? She chose the latter. The increased risks of her coming and going were offset by having less to pack in. She hid until nightfall and then carefully backtracked past the hunting camp to her parked car.

Hiding and waiting, her long night had begun. She'd sleep in the car tonight, well away from the campers. There she'd eat cold food, evacuate her bowels, and restock parka pockets and backpack for the long wait ahead. Her only creature comforts were a waterproof seat cushion and a small tarp.

* * * *

Her wind-up alarm rang two hours before dawn. El relieved herself in the bushes and drank the last tepid coffee from her thermos. She had a flashlight but still needed to bypass the camp using only faint moonlight. With hunters at their spots before sunrise, she had to be in her place when they arrived.

Using the shadows of the tall larch trees, she skirted the quarry. After she had rounded a bend that put her out of sight of the camp, it was finally safe to use her flashlight. It lit a small moving circle on the ground as she went a quarter mile down the old logging road to her sniper's nest.

With one hand free to grasp tree branches to steady herself, El climbed to her perch above and to the left of Hubert's spot. She moved some pre-cut branches to her front as added concealment. Laying out the tarp, El shed her backpack and gently laid down the rifle. She used her cushion as a backrest, propped against the backpack. She placed the canteen, some food items, the pee jar, and toilet paper all within easy and quiet reach.

An hour later, as daylight approached, Hubert arrived and took his expected place. Whatever hunting savvy he may have had in his youth seemed gone when he lit his first of many cigarettes.

Her rifle rested across her lap beneath gloved hands. The stillness of the deep woods amplified the feel of the cold. She squeezed her upper arms to her sides and enjoyed the small momentary extra warmth. She took, cold comfort in the t. *This is still warmer than a winter morning back in Poland.* And she waited for her shot.

What she wanted was an upper torso shot, the most likely fatal wound, at a time when other hunters were firing. The mountains disguised the location of sounds. That's when she'd shoot: if opportunity and auditory cover converged.

The most shots of any morning during the entire season are heard an hour after sunrise on opening day. The animals have just risen from their fern beds. After ten months of not being hunted, their natural caution is at a low ebb.

The sounds of shots came from multiple locations. Sometimes one shot came with a pause before more shots. Sometimes two or more shots came in quick succession. When the first shot rang out, El brought up her rifle and studied Hubert through her four-power Weaver scope.

She had fashioned a rest for her rifle. The stock nestled in the fork of a pine branch so her muscles didn't tire from keeping steady the eight pounds of wood and metal.

When two shots from a distant location rang out, El peered through her scope. Hubert had turned toward the sound of the shots. His flank was now exposed, and she aimed.

She remembered lying prone in the Galilee dust years ago in Israel. El saw herself sighting down the long barrel of her Enfield rifle. She heard from behind her ear the voice of Solomon, a DIN instructor. *Breathe in and let it out slowly. Squeeze the trigger gently as you exhale.*

Halfway through exhaling a breath, her trigger snapped, and a shot rang out. The loud 'crack' and the rifle's recoil went unnoticed as El's adrenaline surged. She refocused the scope on where Hubert had been. He'd vanished. She knew that he'd not left his spot. That, she would have seen. No, he was down. The only question was, '*Is he dead?*' Her shot was aimed for the center of his upper torso just under his left armpit. Wounding the big German or worse yet, ventilating his parka in a cloud of feather filling would be bad.

The patient huntress cleared the spent shell from her rifle and pocketed the brass case, leaving no trace of her nest. She chambered another round into her .270. Later she would scatter the branches used for cover and rough up the ground where she'd waited.

El kept her scope trained on where Hubert had gone down, watching for a telltale stir of branches or some other sign that her prey was only wounded. Other distant shots rang out, the better to disguise hers. Five minutes, fifteen, and still she watched. If her shot had been true, it would have exploded his heart or lungs. Either wound would have been fatal.

El knew her choice had to be made. Leave now, or check the body? Was the certainty of his death worth the price of perhaps losing the believability of an accidental shooting? Her mind approached the question, but always backed away, from a final decision.

Instead El continued to watch, avoiding the choice. *I can't get out of here until sunset anyway, since I don't know where Duano and Curtis are sitting.* As she watched for signs of life, her mind went down a checklist of considerations. *If Hubert doesn't show up back at camp tonight, what will they do? When? Sunset? Or will they wait a bit?* El's best guess was that when the Nazi was a no-show, Duano would go out to Hubert's spot to find out why.

Has he fallen and was hurt? Fallen asleep? Smuggled out Schnapps and was drunk? These were the questions she imagined Duano would ask himself. But he would investigate, of that she had no doubt.

She checked her scope again. No signs of life at the one-hour mark. Still she watched and waited. Indecision was its own trap. Planning and preparation could only go so far. Sometimes risk was unavoidable, just as long as it was not needless risk. Her decision made, she peered around carefully, then stood up and stepped out from her blind towards Hubert.

Gun at the ready, she advanced on the Nazi's position. Trees and forest shadows hid her approach. El stopped before crossing the dead yellow grass cover on the old logging road. She crouched down, studying Hubert's spot. From there she could see the brown and loden green mass of a body. Raising her rifle, she checked for any rise and fall of the figure's chest; a twitch perhaps, or hands that uncurled. No signs of life appeared. "I got him," she whispered aloud. Her course now clear, she backtracked to her former spot and restored the site as best she could.

It was just before mid-day and the October sun lightened a cloudless blue sky. The overnight frost had gone, and the air was now a tolerable 40 degrees. She'd wait until just before sunset to head out along her practiced escape route.

* * * *

Duano and Curtis would be back at camp by sunset. A campfire needed to be built, dinner started, and the first drinks of the day poured.

El's timing allowed her to move toward camp without having an unexpected encounter with Duano or Curtis. As before, she'd wait for an opportunity to pass their camp unnoticed. Tonight, she hoped her chance would come when the two went in search of Hubert.

She crouched in the shadows and observed the camp. Curtis was first to arrive. Ten minutes later Duano walked in. Twilight was overtaking the site.

"Did you see any game today?"

Curtis shook his head.

Duano laid his rifle down, careful to protect the sighting of his scope. Not yet ready to begin the evening chores of building a fire and making dinner, he picked up the Jack Daniel's whiskey bottle.

"Let's wait for Hub," suggested Curtis.

While they waited, a common courtesy between partners at hunting camp, Duano built a fire and Curtis began to work on dinner. Twenty minutes passed. The evening fire lit, the men relaxed on log rounds by the rock-encircled firepit.

"He's late." A note of worry had crept into Curtis's voice. Duano stared into the flames as the fire popped and wood smoke drifted with the wind in his direction.

"Yeah, I think we might want to take a walk out to his spot. I haven't heard any shooting since this morning, but he might have an animal down and can't leave until he's got it opened up to cool out."

Curtis answered by rising and putting on his parka. "Let's go look."

Duano and Curtis took their flashlights and guns with them. The lights were for searching if needed. The guns were for protection from an unexpected meeting with a bear or cougar. Or perhaps to shoot any wandering elk they might encounter on the trail. Duano led the way down the left-hand trail from camp.

When the two hunters were out of view, El left her hiding spot. Staying at the edge of the clearing so as not to leave telltale footprints in camp, she walked the 30 yards to the road and headed the final 100 yards to her car.

* * * *

As the two hunters approached the spot where Hubert was supposed to be, they saw nothing and no one. Then Curtis noticed the loden green lump lying on the cut-bank above the grass-covered trail. He signaled to Duano and headed off the logging road to Hubert's probable location.

Hubert had long gone cold to the touch, but his body had not been disturbed by scavengers. He lay on his right side and a single bullet hole was visible on the left side of the green parka.

"Ah shit, somebody's shot hit him." Curtis spat onto the forest floor. They both went silent, trying to decide the right thing to do.

"Should we bring the body back to camp or leave it undisturbed until the Shoshone County Sheriff can arrive?"

Curtis shrugged his shoulders. "Man, this is a mess. I was just starting to like the guy; even if he was a kraut."

"I didn't know him. If Millie wasn't about to have the baby, I'd probably never have met him," said Duano.

"Well, no one back at the church is gonna be happy about this. Nope, no one is going to like this a bit. There have been too many God-damn accidents, and now this, and while he's with me. Shit-shit shit."

Between the choices, the latter meant one of them had to stay the night to protect the body from predators. They chose the first option. Trying to be as respectful of the body as possible, they took turns packing Hubert out in a fireman's carry. Big in life, Hubert was heavy in death, so his remains were repeatedly passed back and forth, as was his rifle.

Back at camp, they draped the body over the hood of the car like they would an elk. When Duano looked at this tableau, he had second ts. "Nah, we can't do that," and they moved Hubert to the back seat. There he lay as they packed up and drove over the Hobo Pass and down to the road along the St. Joe River.

When they connected with a state highway outside the town of St. Maries, they had to make a decision whether to take Hubert to the local Benewah Sheriff's Office in that town. Duano stopped his car and turned to Curtis.

"What's it gonna be? Here or drive the 70 miles to the Sheriff in Wallace?"

"I don't think it matters to Hubert but it sure as hell does matter to me. I just want to get him out, get a drink and get home."

Duano made a guess as to which way to go to find some all-night law enforcement. He drove through downtown St. Maries until he saw a blue, "Hospital" sign. If that didn't get them to the sheriff, at least any Emergency Room would have directions. With the hospital in sight, they both saw a lighted sign, "Sheriff's Office."

In the full dark of the October night, Duano followed the only light high above the outside stairs to the night-time Sheriff's Office on the second floor. It was locked. He rang the doorbell next to the green metal door. The peep hole darkened, and an inquiring eye appeared. Then the door opened out onto the landing, forcing Duano to step aside. Standing in the doorway was Deputy Ben Christian, who looked at the two hunters, waiting for one of them to speak.

"I'm Curtis Taylor and this is Duano Lagomarsino. We're from up in Kootenai County. We were hunting with our partner, Hubert Schwarz, over the ridge at Yellow Jacket Butte. When he didn't show up at camp tonight, we went out to his spot and found him. He was dead. We've got him in our car. Where do you want Hubert?"

"Now hold on a minute. You've got a body in your car? Is that what you're telling me?"

"Well, yes. We didn't think it was right to leave him out there overnight. We didn't know what might happen to him."

"But he was already dead?"

Duano hung back, content to let Curtis do the talking.

'Well, yes he is, but we didn't do it. It looks like a stray bullet got him. We went looking when he didn't show up for our first 'Jack' of the night."

"Where's your car?"

Both hunters pointed to the parking lot below. "Well you boys had best come in and take a seat while I get Sheriff Kurtz out of bed. He's gonna want to talk to you both." Then as an after-t Deputy Christian asked, "Is the car locked?"

"Well, no. We didn't think anyone would try to steal Hubert. But we locked up our rifles safe in the trunk."

After a long night, Duano and Curtis were released, but Hubert stayed in St. Maries.

26. Crossroads

Driving home in the dark, El took her time negotiating the twisty mountain road. As she went, her mind worked on how to get rid of the murder weapon. A plan emerged by the time she arrived back in Bayview.

The next day she went into action. She heaved the rifle bolt out of sight into the mouth of the snake den behind her cabin. She removed the wooden gun stock and burned it in her fireplace. Next, she unscrewed the scope from the barrel assembly to keep for future use. The unique pattern of lands and grooves inside the rifle barrel could be matched to a particular bullet, so it had to go.

Without access to a machine shop where the barrel could be cut up or flattened, at the bottom of an 1100-foot-deep lake was the best available option.

At lunch with Millie, El shared the outcome of her hunt and her further need.

"I took him with one shot. Got out unseen and made it home. I've disposed of some of the pieces of my rifle, but I need a boat to get out to the deepest part of the lake. That's where I'll drop the gun barrel."

Millie chewed her sandwich, not having an immediate answer or even a suggestion.

"Can you hide the barrel until we can dump it?"

"Good idea, but we aren't out of the woods until that barrel is at the bottom of the lake." They had no quick solution, only a shared awareness of the importance of solving this last riddle.

Two days later, several local papers carried Hubert's obituary. The obits also quoted the Coroner's Inquest conclusion of "accidental death by gunshot." In their review, the facts of the event—caliber of the bullet being that of a common hunting weapon, the timing of the death being opening morning of elk season, and the place of death being an active elk hunting area—all supported the accidental death conclusion.

* * * *

While putting away laundry, Millie was alone with her ts. Her fingers touched the Boker straight razor, sleeping in the bottom of her lingerie drawer. She had neither looked at the blade nor thought about it for a long time. It brought back so many memories, all bad. There and then she resolved to remove it from her life. She asked El if her blade could share a long, dreamless sleep with the rifle barrel.

"I think my life has moved on and God, I hope I'm right."

El took the straight razor with her and hid it in the woods. It lay together with the .270 barrel and trigger assembly until a boat could be arranged. Millie decided to see if she could get the use of a boat for El.

* * * *

"Honey, do you know if the station has any small boats for day use? Recreational toys for station people to use on their days off, like water skis? I've never been out on the lake at all. I'd like to see what it's like. Can you see what's available?"

At the dinner table that night Duano announced, "I've got us a fourteen-foot boat for the weekend. It's actually a supply transfer boat I use when we need to deliver parts out to something afloat."

"Does it have a sail, a motor or what?"

"It has a small outboard motor. I'll bring it to the public dock in town after work this Friday. It's ours for the weekend. If you pack a lunch, I'll take you out for a cruise on Saturday. I'm thinking we should get a sitter for baby Rosie."

"That sounds wonderful. I'll see if El can watch her god-daughter." She'd pass the news to El tomorrow at lunch. This left the assassin three days' time to come up with a plan using the boat to sink the final vestiges of two murders.

"I'll steal the boat Saturday night," was the essence of El's plan. "We don't know where the deepest spot is. But if it's 100 feet just off the dock here, then anywhere out towards the middle will be deep enough."

* * * *

Millie said that her first boat ride anywhere was wonderful. The November weather was cold as they motored along under the clear blue sky. They headed up the lake to sights only available from the water. Few roads came down to the lakeshore until the north end where the towns of Sagle and Sandpoint sat.

El planned to paddle out and not risk the noise of the outboard. Unsure if the boat had an emergency paddle, she bought her own from an out-of-town source, just in case. Her back-up plan, if challenged, was to claim that Millie had given her permission to use the boat. Duano could plead ignorance, and Millie could plead forgetfulness.

Saturday night was moonless. El had located a spot on the lake front near her cabin where the shore was in reach from a passing boat. She paddled the quarter mile out of town to her spot, previously marked by a white tablecloth she'd tied up like so much laundry.

There she took aboard the rifle barrel assembly and razor. She paddled out to the middle of the water. Over the side the two pieces of metal went, sinking into the blue-black depths of the lake. Then El rowed back to the town dock, all traces of her weapon and Millie's now far away.

One week later, and right on time, Millie's second baby entered the world. They named her Lena in honor of Lena Olson, who'd helped her so much when she'd arrived in Keyport. Their two-bedroom house was now full. Millie would either have to start sleeping with both feet in a two-gallon bucket or they'd need a bigger house. As Lena had once warned Millie, Duano was as horny as a two-peckered billygoat.

* * * *

The day after Baby Lena's birth, El slept in, enjoying her newly found peace of mind and the bright reflected sun off the snow-covered ground. Her first stop was to visit Frank Gagliardi at the restaurant. Frank would be doing prep-work for tonight's dinner, already dressed in his Chef's whites.

"Hey, we need to talk. I've been doing a lot of thinking, and it involves you." She kissed the silent man's cheek. "Can we get together tonight after your dinner service?"

"Sure, but if you want me to stop now, I will. Is everything OK? Do you need me to do something? Just tell me what you want."

El smiled at his immediate, kind, and concerned response. "After work is better, actually. What time?"

"A weeknight shouldn't be busy, so I'll close the kitchen at nine and leave my crew to clean. Will you have eaten? I can bring us a late dinner?"

"No, you are all I need."

Frank put down the knife in his hand and reached out. "Should I worry? Are you all right?"

She always marveled at the man's empathy and concern. He was dealing with so many demons of his own. She squeezed his hand a long moment before letting go.

"I'm fine, and my demons are all asleep. I'll see you about ten." El turned and departed the kitchen. Only later did she notice the pungent smell of garlic lingering on her fingers.

* * * *

Frank knocked on her cabin door. His car's engine pinged as the hot metal cooled in the fall night air. He'd brought a good bottle of Italian red wine. El opened her door, took her lover by the hand and kissed him. He gave her a one-armed hug in return. She pointed to her couch and together they sat.

"Shall I open our wine?"

"Maybe later," El replied.

If she refused wine, Frank knew that something important was about to come up. He waited for her to start the conversation.

"It's done. All of my demons are now in their own dreamless sleep. I've been killing people since I was eighteen and I'm tired of killing." Silent now, she squeezed his hand and saw that his eyes were focused on the floor.

"There's something else," and her eyes focused on the blank wall. "I felt ashamed every time he touched me, and I didn't fight him. I did nothing." Her voice went silent, but neither spoke. Finally, El continued. "This is my door to a tomorrow with you and I want to step through it, if you'll be there on the other side. I want to share a life, make a new life, and not take life anymore."

"I don't want to kill any more either, not ever. What do you want, then?" asked Frank. He shifted his eyes from the floor to her face.

"I want you and I want to have your baby. I've shared my demons with you. And that's something I've never done, not with anybody. You understand me?"

"Yes, I do." Then he paused, moving his gaze from El's face to the floor and back. "Because we know each other's demons. I'm so glad that you are finding peace."

They sat silent. Only sounds from the quiet night intruded in their long silence.

"All I can promise is that I will protect you from everything and everybody who haunts you, if you'll do the same for me. I love you," Frank said.

El found her eyes welling up.

As her tears began to fall, he waited patiently. When she remained silent, he added; "I love you too. If you'll have me, I want to marry you."

El sniffed back her tears before answering. "Yes"

"We can pick out a ring in town tomorrow."

"Maybe someday, but all I want now or ever is what the Nazis took away from me, a family. I don't need the ring."

Frank knelt and picked her up in his strong arms, carrying her to bed. No other words passed their lips that night.

In the morning over coffee as they looked out on the clean, cold vista of lake and forest, El asked, "Can I have a dog?"

Something has relit her fire. She really is looking ahead, to me, to us. The Nazis couldn't break her spirit, even if it bent.

"Yes, if we can move to Coeur d' Alene and get a place with a yard. That's closer to Luigi's. What kind of dog do you want?"

"Any kind, as long as it's not a German Shepherd."

27.   A Blast from the Past, May 1954

Millie picked up the mail from their box at the post office every day on her way home from the store. Among the five letters in their box today was one addressed to Mr. and Mrs. D. Lagomarsino from P. McBride. Not even waiting to reach home, she opened the letter there in the small lobby.

> Dear Duano and Millie,
> Good news for me, if not for you. I am traveling east by train on business this coming June. The route takes me through Spokane, and I'd love to visit you, if the timing allows. The Burlington Northern schedule shows we have a six-hour layover at the Spokane station. Something about changing engines for the next leg of the trip.
> We pull in at 9 A.M. on 6/1 and leave at 2 P.M. that same afternoon. I don't know where the Spokane station is, but I'm sure you'll have no trouble finding it. Please tell me if we can get together in town and I'll take us all to lunch. My Pam isn't along on this trip, but she sends her love to you both. Hope to hear from you,
> Pat McBride.

Pat's letter, rather than filling her with joy, filled Millie with dread. What if one niggling detail he might share didn't fit the narrative she'd concocted eight years ago? So much more was at risk for her now. She was a married woman, the mother of two daughters and living in a place she loved. What if the wrong word made a lie of her life and she was divorced and shamed? Had she thrown away her straight razor too soon? At the very least, her

209

fears would be constant companions until Pat traveled on from Spokane on his journey east.

* * * *

When Duano saw the letter at dinner that night, his immediate joy matched Millie's concealed apprehension.

"This is great. I love this guy. We got each other through the tough, lonely times."

She smiled in agreement and returned to nursing baby Lena.

"He's not much of a letter writer. He and Pam are still in their Victorian house across the street from Delores Park in San Francisco. He's been back with the Southern Pacific railroad since the war ended."

"Do they have children?"

"No kids, just the two of them. Jeez, that's such a short layover. I'd like to show him the station. With his background from Keyport, Mare Island, and with the railroad, I bet he'd be interested to see what we do."

Millie's barely concealed fear came welling up into her throat. A few hours with Pat in Spokane was risky enough but days together and all the things that could go wrong was almost too much. A single wrong word or the smallest accidental slip by Pat could mean disaster. Involuntarily her body tensed. This was unnoticed by Duano, but her clenching subtly communicated itself to baby Lena. The baby stopped her nursing, unlatched from the breast and began to cry.

Millie forced herself to relax. "Do you think you could get him on station? With all the secret stuff going on over there, would they allow him?" Four-month-old Lena resumed nursing, unconcerned about anything but

Millie's milk and the warmth and safety of her mother's arms.

"Hmm, good question. We've got a month until he'll be arriving. I'll talk to Master Chief Norris tomorrow. Norris knows Charlie Olson and their counterpart at Mare Island. I'm guessing something can be arranged."

Millie nodded as she struggled to hold the baby and eat with her one free hand. She'd serve nothing requiring cutting ever again if she was nursing.

"His time in Spokane isn't enough for a good visit with us, let alone to see the station. I wonder if he might stay over for a night or two? Catch the next train to wherever?" Duano drummed the fingers of his free hand on the tabletop as he verbalized his ts.

"Ok, I see that, but where would we put him? Our couch isn't very welcoming for a special guest."

As her husband contemplated this last wrinkle Millie had another t. "How about this dear, since you don't like to write letters. Suppose I write back tomorrow and suggest that Pat try to arrange a short layover in Spokane. We'll pick him up and bring him back for the next train."

"So, where does he stay?"

"We can afford to pay for a room in Coeur d' Alene. We'll take him for a tour of Bayview, meet the daughters, maybe a lake cruise and of course a dinner at Luigi's on the Lake. I'll get El to take care of the kids, so we have a nice adult visit. How does that sound to you?"

"I like it. Go ahead with your plan and meanwhile I'll see if I can get him cleared for a tour of the Bayview station."

Armed with her husband's approval, she crafted a message hidden in plain sight within her letter. Since Pat knew Millie's truths, she hoped he would recognize the coaching about not pointing out her necessary lies. Three drafts later, Millie sent off the note.

Dear Patrick,

It thrills Duano and me that you will pass our way. We can meet you at the station, but here's an idea for you to consider. We live a good hour from Spokane and want to show you the beauty of our area. It is wonderful. We want you to meet our daughters and as many of our good friends as time allows. Also, Duano is trying to get you a pass onto the Bayview station. Like Keyport, access is limited, but he thinks for someone as special as you, he can arrange it.

Anyway, we'd like you to see if travel options would permit you to have at least a two-day lay-over. If you can swing that, we'll arrange the rest. Since the three of us have never sat down together, we might be sharing how you stopped in the butcher shop where I was clerking. I've never forgotten how you listened to my hopes and dreams of getting out of Dorris and finding better, more suitable work. I'll always be in your debt for the opportunity you provided me. Now, married with two girls, I owe it all to you. I'm sure that Duano feels the same.

Please see if you can arrange the extra time.

Love, Millie.

Now Millie had to hope that Pat recognized her message for what it was—a plea.

* * * *

Ten days later, they got another letter.

> Dear Folks,
> Thanks so much for the generous offer. I can't change the date of my convention, but I can come a few days early and still leave at 2 P.M. on 6/1 like before. I'll take you up on your offer. My new arrival is 9 A.M. on 5/30. I'm looking forward to seeing the both of you, meeting Rosie and Lena and sharing the beauty of what you folks see daily.
> Happy trails,
> Pat.

With no clue about whether he had recognized Millie's hidden message, she was left to worry about what his visit might mean for her.

She shared Pat's letter with Duano that night. He was working on getting permission for a special tour. Millie volunteered to arrange a hotel room in Coeur d' Alene for the night of 5/30 through the morning of 6/1.

* * * *

At 7 A.M. on May 30th, Millie handed off the girls to Aunt El. Duano took time off from work and they rode together to the Spokane train station.

Her fear of what Pat might reveal had not diminished, but lacking an alternative, she'd smiled and kept on with her routine. As they waited for the train, Millie fought back the nausea that was betraying her anxiety.

When Pat stepped down from the train, they were on the platform to greet him. He grabbed Duano in a bear hug and got strong male back slaps in return.

"It's good to see you, brother," Pat said as the men released each other to arms' length. So far Millie was ignored. *Why is he ignoring me?*

"I've got my same pigskin bag from Keyport in the baggage car. Let me get that and we can go."

To announce her presence, Millie asked. "Did they feed you breakfast on the train?" Now conscious of his error, Pat turned to her with a smile and a hug.

"I could eat a horse."

Fighting down her internal butterflies, Millie replied. "I'm sorry, we have no horse."

Both men chuckled, and they all headed down the platform toward the baggage car, visible four cars ahead, as it disgorged freight and suitcases. When Pat's brown pigskin bag appeared, Duano picked it up and led the way to their car.

They stopped for a hearty breakfast at Molly's Diner before leaving Spokane. Pat and Duano kept up a non-stop conversation about mutual friends and shared experiences. They moved on to sharing changes in their lives during the intervening years since Duano had visited San Francisco in the spring of 1946. By accident, design or just lost in the moment with an old friend, Pat neither said nor did anything to raise or lower Millie's fears. She was just along for the ride.

Their drive back to Bayview was a leisurely guided tour. She rode in the back seat as the two men talked and laughed all the way. Duano took them on a circuitous route, starting with a brief stop at Spokane Falls. On they went, east through the little town of Post Falls and into

Coeur d' Alene. The three stopped at the same Coeur d' Alene beach where Duano and Millie had waded and watched the tug back when they arrived in 1946. As they stood by the water's edge, Duano got down to the business of how Pat wanted to spend his time.

"Millie and I have the things outlined that we thought you might like. I'll run down what's on our list. Now nothing is chiseled in stone, so if you hear anything you'd like to skip, say so." And he launched into the planned itinerary.

"Hold on, partner. Whatever you decided is fine. Let's go!"

First, they made a stop at the Coeur d' Alene hotel for Pat to check in and leave his bag. Then they drove to Bayview to see the house. Meeting the daughters and lunch beside the lake were next.

Duano had arranged a station tour for Pat. Master Chief Norris had become aware of Pat's considerable help to Keyport and the FBI. Norris also knew about Pat's help in managing the truth about Colin Kelly.

The myth of Colin Kelly's heroism right after Pearl Harbor was considered necessary by the government during the dark days of 1942. The public was given the story that Kelly's B-17 bomber had destroyed a Japanese cruiser in Manila Bay by dropping a bomb down its smokestack. In truth, no ship had been destroyed before the plane was shot down. But, for the good of the war effort, Duano had kept the secret.

Not only was Pat welcome, but Master Chief Norris wanted to meet him and lead his tour. Pat was very much an honored guest and got an insider's look at the research station. While Millie was home with the babies, the three men shared a toast, bourbon from a bottle that appeared from Norris's bottom drawer.

After the Bayview tour, Duano and Pat picked up Millie again. She'd arranged a two-day baby sitting with Chief Norris's teenage daughter. The three of them drove to Coeur d' Alene for an adults-only dinner at Frank and El's house. They had acquired a nice craftsman bungalow on the lakeshore next to Tubb's Hill Park. Still not married, Frank and El had been living blissfully in sin since the first of the year.

They ended the evening with dropping Pat off at his hotel in Coeur d' Alene.

* * * *

The next morning the three met for breakfast in town and then took a noon lake cruise. During the three hours on the lake they bought snacks and drinks at the on-board bar.

After the lake cruise, Pat went to his hotel to rest and change. Duano and Millie went back to El's house where they changed clothes and relaxed on the back deck. At 5:00 P.M. the Lagomarsinos and El picked up Pat at his hotel.

That evening a special sunset dinner at Luigi's on the Lake, prepared by Chef Frank, brought Pat's visit to a close. Brizz and his wife, Sophia, toasted the group with their own home-made grappino. After that they lingered on the restaurant's deck until time and alcohol took their toll and brought the evening to an end.

When he walked Pat into his hotel's lobby, Duano clarified the plan for the next morning.

"Millie will take you to the train. I'm due back at work, so we'll say our goodbyes tonight. She'll pick you up at 7

A.M. You'll have breakfast together and then drive to the station. Okay?"

"Fine."

They turned to face each other for a final handshake. Duano did not release his friend's hand. "We have both been there for each other when needed. You took care of me when I got hit by the drunk driver after our Christmas Dinner."

"You helped me try to get Bea out of the camp. The messages you used with your cousin to get information about how she was doing. The money you loaned me for the bribe. It all meant the world to me then, and it always will."

"Friends, pisanos for life, right?"

"Absolutely. Oh, and thank you for whatever you did or didn't do about the guard, Gladney: the one who attacked Bea and robbed me."

They parted as the best possible friends. Millie hung back from the parting. She stayed on tenterhooks, suppressing nausea all the time, waiting for the one wrong word to be said.

* * * *

She arrived at Pat's hotel at 7 A.M., and he loaded his single pigskin bag into the car. She'd chosen a particular coffee shop for their breakfast. Her choice had booths instead of open tables. They entered and ordered before Millie started her long-dreaded conversation. It was now or never. She couldn't live any longer, filling every day with her fear of discovery. Steeling herself, she raised her eyes from the tabletop and let fly.

"He doesn't know about my past. That secret has stayed buried because no one challenged my lies about how or where we met. I can't live with the worry, Pat. Is he going to find out from you?"

"No, he's not, and he never will."

Millie reached across the table and took Pat's hand. She tried to speak but her throat had thickened.

Pat leaned closer. "When we met, my sins had already exceeded anything that you could ever do. You just didn't know it." He reached across the table taking her other hand in his.

"When I returned the next day, I knew all my sins had done me no good. I'd lost the woman I'd come to save. I would have paid any price, but it didn't matter to her." He stopped as their waitress approached with two plates. "We'll talk more in the car."

They ate their eggs and potatoes in silence except for Millie's heartfelt response. "Thank you...thank you."

After they'd eaten and once back driving, Pat sensed the tension that had left Millie and now he knew why.

"I got the message from your letter. I thought your clue was brilliant. You worked in sort of a meat market. You sold to retail customers."

Millie turned off the car radio and pulled the car over. Foot on the brake, at the side of the road, she turned to Pat. When she tried to speak, no words came out, so she turned off the ignition and waited until the waves of emotion passed.

Pat turned to her. "I'm sorry. I wasn't trying to be funny so much as just lighten the mood. But I am sorry that I didn't realize you worried all these years about your past being discovered. I'm so sorry that I didn't respond to the clue in your letter and put your mind at ease."

"It's all right, my fears were just my own. I should never have doubted you in any way."

"What I wanted for you that day was what you've got now. Don't you see my wish for you came true?"

"It did, it did. I found a wonderful man. I have a home, friends, and two beautiful daughters." Millie paused but had to ask another other long held question. "Did you plan for me to meet Duano?"

"When I came back to you that day, it was the low point of my life. I wasn't thinking at all, except about the woman I'd lost and mistakes I'd made. Now I'm glad you did meet. It delighted me when I got the news you two were getting married. But I can't claim credit for any of the good things that you yourself have done since then."

When Millie could finally drive, she turned to Pat, wiping her eyes. "We'd better go, or I'll make you miss your train."

On they drove, through the town of Post Falls and across the state line into Washington.

The sign along the highway read "Spokane City Limits." Millie pointed it out to Pat and only then as they neared the station did he speak.

"Listen, enough of this. You are free from your past. That was my gift to you then. I'm going to give you another gift now. Forgive yourself. You've earned it. You survived and only did what you had to do. What you've built for Duano—his home, a family and the unconditional support—more than make up for anything you ever did."

Pat hadn't shared any more of his own darkness with Millie then. But now she knew that she'd helped him as assuredly as he'd helped her.

At the station, Pat took his single suitcase from the trunk and they parted.

"Love to Duano," he called over his shoulder.

She responded, "Love to Pam."

Millie took home with her a second gift from Pat McBride: self-forgiveness.

* * * *

"How did the drive go?" Duano sat at the dining room table. Rosie perched on her booster seat and fiddled with the mixed vegetables on her plate. Baby Lena occupied a highchair near Millie, who helped the little one practice holding her own bottle as the first step in learning to feed herself.

"Oh, fine. I got Pat to the station on time and we had a nice visit on the drive over."

"Good. Thanks for driving. I'm glad we all got to spend time together.

"Oh, one more thing"

"What's that?"

"We're going to need a bigger house. You're going to be a daddy again."

Duano's face broke out in a huge smile which turned into uproarious laughter as he rose from his dinner and encircled Millie's shoulders with his strong arms.

"This is wonderful! God, I love you." His laughter subsided as he kissed the nape of her neck. "Tomorrow,

I'll start checking with our housing office for a three-bedroom house here in Bayview."

"If it's a boy, I think we should name him Patrick," suggested Millie

* * * *

It was the warmest day of April 1955. The mothers and their preschoolers were enjoying the early spring sun. After the cold of a North Idaho winter, the balmy 60-degree day was a magnet for parents and children to get outside. Ten different blankets lay under the mottled light that filtered down through tall red firs. From their picnic spot, the Pend Oreille lakeshore was visible across a dirt road, spread out as a deep blue background panorama.

Millie and her girls were one of the families enjoying the annual 'Little Angels Nursery School' picnic. Rosie's god-mother El, now pregnant with her first child, had come out from Coeur d' Alene. Four-year-old Rosie played with six of her age mates. The fallen red fir cones morphed into balls, some juggled while others were gleefully tossed or traded.

Seventeen-month-old Lena practiced her newly acquired skill, walking. Both girls were in sight, as seven-months pregnant Millie sat beside eight-month pregnant El. The two women visited and read under the early afternoon sun.

"Andrea, Andrea, come away from the road, honey."

There was no note of worry in the mother's call. Just another of the many Mommies giving directions from among the picnickers. Millie, with two children of her own, empathized with Loretta Story, who had to keep simultaneous watch on her two-, three-, and four-year-olds. Andrea seemed a likely poster girl for 'The Terrible Twos.'

"Andrea NO." This time Loretta sounded worried.

Millie put down her book and began looking around for the runaway toddler. A split second later the loud sounds of worry changed to screams of panic.

"Andrea—Andrea—Andrea!" Instinctively all the other mothers froze. Feedings, changing diapers and the simultaneous supervision of multiple children all stopped. Loretta Story was on her feet and rushing towards the road separating the picnic area from the lakeshore.

Andrea had vanished from sight.

Loretta rushed to the water's edge while other mothers screamed to their own young.

"Come to Mommy; stay here on the blanket." Commands to children erupted from multiple mothers.

Millie did the same, hugging baby Lena to her side as she called Rosie back. Feeling like a beached whale as she negotiated the ever more difficult job of standing up, Millie struggled to her feet.

"Rosie you stay here on our blanket with Auntie El and don't let go of your sister. Mommy will be right back."

"Andrea!" Loretta was screaming in full panic mode as she stood on the bank inches away from the crystal-clear lake water, the doll-like shape of her toddler still moving below the lake's surface.

Loretta's screams were now for help, as she watched the little life slip away before her eyes.

Millie lumbered to the lake and grabbed the screaming Loretta.

"I can't swim," moaned the weeping mother as she pointed into the deep, cold water.

Neither can I, thought Millie as she jumped into the cold, clear depths of Pend Oreille. In graceless motion, her flailing limbs drew her down to the still-struggling toddler. Millie pulled the child to her breast and rolled over with her face now turned towards the sunny surface, fifteen feet above.

Non-swimmer that she was, Millie had not filled her lungs before jumping. But neither had she exhaled as she struggled to dive.

Don't worry baby, you're not alone. Momma's got you. My God the sun is beautiful. Unstuck in time and floating with the toddler in her arms, Millie had no more ts as she waited for her burning lungs to trade their air for water.

Whether through God's plan or tful evolution over millennia, Millie's pregnancy had increased her buoyancy. As she rose, three other mothers stood along the shoreline with Loretta.

When Millie's face broke the surface, Naomi Marcus jumped in. The baby was handed up to the shore where trained women began life-saving procedures. Next Naomi, with two quick strokes, reached the shore with Millie. Many hands helped the two from the cold waters up onto the shore. An exhausted Millie stayed where she lay. A picnic blanket covered her, and she closed her eyes.

* * * *

Duano was asleep at her bedside when Millie awoke that night. Her hand was still clutched in his and she was aware this was a hospital and not home. *Let him sleep or wake him up?* She squeezed her husband's hand.

"I'm back."

Enclosing her in his strong arms, Duano whispered in her ear. "Please don't do that again."

"Sorry, it must have been the Mommy gene."

The End

Epilogue

In September 1998, a woman and her son who were driving past the church had their car shot at by compound guards who mistook automobile backfires for gunshots. They were shot at and chased down by Aryan Nations church guards, beaten and detained at gunpoint.

A Civil jury found the church and its leader grossly negligent in selecting and overseeing the two guards. The couple was awarded $6.3 million in damages.

On October 31, 2000, two days after the last White Pride Parade that drew twenty attendees, and days before the church was to surrender the twenty-acre compound to the plaintiff, its founder filed for Bankruptcy Court protection. The property was transferred to the plaintiff's in February 2001. The 20 acres were repurchased was ultimately donated to a local college foundation as a Peace Park. All the former church buildings were removed.

Acknowledgements

The first people to thank are my volunteer readers: Dave Gressard, Monique Lillard, Dave Quinn, Monica Ray and Louise Regelin. Also, thanks to my copy wrangler Gordon Long who fights mightily to keep my point-of-view straight. It was a dirty job, Gordon, but somebody had to do it. Special thanks to my wife of 46 years, Susan, who is my consultant on all things feminine.

From the Author

Here are the bones of my story. I have changed the names to protect the guilty.

Eleanor's DIN activity is based on my first clue about the DIN's existence. That awareness came from the autobiography of the writer we know as John le Carre. Through it, I discovered Michael Elkins book, *Forged in Fury.* From that book I also learned about the DIN and the *Werwolfs.*

My contacts with the Aryans of north Idaho were extensive. Beginning in October 1981 and for the next 10 years, I was the one and only Resident Agent in that area for the Federal District Court and the United States Parole Commission. I handled the ten northern counties of Idaho. This area included Spirit Lake, Coeur d' Alene and Bayview, Idaho.

I first went to the Aryan Nations church compound in 1982, after a former Grand Dragon of the Texas Ku Klux Klan, wanted on federal charges, was found hiding there. This was my first interview with the reverend who founded the church. Our contacts continued for years and included my investigations and his supervision during the lead-up to his trial at Fort Smith, Arkansas, on a charge of sedition.

The real Aryan church survived for portions of three decades, from the mid-1970's through the mid 1990's. Their annual 'White Pride Parade' in downtown Coeur d' Alene, Idaho, and their display of Nazi flags and uniforms were a source of embarrassment to the larger community.

Their offshoot, 'The Order' came and went through three iterations, each as violent as its predecessors. The original Order robbed banks and armored Brinks trucks, getting away with over $3.4 million dollars. They were finally brought down by an insider turned federal witness. Seventy-eight individuals were ultimately charged in related federal cases. The founder of 'The Order' died in a stand-off with the FBI at his home on Whidbey Island, Washington.

I investigated and supervised two of the eight founding members of The Order. One of its founders was my case when he was arrested for passing counterfeit money. It was then that I interviewed Robert Matthews, the founder of The Order.

The Order II's idea, besides robbing banks, was to steal automatic weapons from multiple Idaho National Guard Armories. Their plans were thwarted by one of their members who became a federal informant.

About The Order II, I investigated and supervised the participant who became an informant. I also did the sentencing reports on the involved husband-and-wife members who were former Sheriff's deputies. My involvement continued as I supervised the wife during her term of probation.

The Order III detonated several bombs, including one at an adult bookstore. They were stopped before carrying out the bombing of a gay bar in Seattle during its business hours. I was first to identify one of its key players whom I had previously supervised on probation for having sent a threatening letter to a state judge.

Please forgive some of the language that I routinely heard and my description of their "Running Nigger" target, which I have seen. The location and description of the church compound are correct to the best of my recollection and research.

Spirit Lake's unusual clay bottom is real, as is its continuing problems with sink holes, the largest of which can drain 30,000 gallons of water per day.

If you want to read more about Pat McBride and Duano Lagomarsino, check out Prisoners of War below.

About the Author

After returning from the Air Force, Stu Scott worked as staff in a juvenile detention facility, moving on to adult probation and finally to federal probation and parole. Simultaneously, in 1980 he returned to the military as a reserve agent with the Army Criminal Investigation Command. Born and raised in the San Francisco bay area, he has lived with his wife in Moscow, Idaho since 1981. Believing that we only go around once in life and that one job is never enough, his other careers include: professional winemaker, college instructor, director of a school for disabled children and as a stained-glass artist.

sls@turbonet.com

Just as a bonus, here is a free short story.

Dreaming

Bruce found himself trying to explain the unexplainable and the unknowable to his office mate. "It must have been Alan Watts and *The Way of Zen* or too much time in the Student Union building at San Francisco State. Maybe it was too much fun in Haight-Ashbury during the 60's. Anyway, a Buddhist I became. I'll admit the California hippie version is 'Buddhism-light.' I don't see our creator as a person but as a force, part of the very universe itself.

"Picture a burning sparkler. The brilliant white light that leaves an afterimage on our retinas is the over-soul, and the sparks flying away are the souls about to enter new bodies for another ride around the great Mandala, our circle of life. For us, birth and death are but two different beaches on the same sea. By virtue of good deeds our souls can be reborn. Our task, through many lives, is to conquer the demands our egos place on us. When we finally manage to separate our soul from the demands, we can find absolute rest."

"So, when I get a new body, I get another chance to polish my soul through good deeds? Sort of like scraping spiritual shit off my shoes?" Don held eye contact with the bubbles in his glass, then added; "So, how about those Giants." The conversation was over.

* * * *

Back home, Walter Cronkite's face filled Bruce's TV screen. "Science and the spiritual met today in San

Francisco. Researchers have unlocked the brain-wave patterns of infants still in their mother's wombs. At 23 weeks the brain waves of unborn babies demonstrate rapid eye movements or REM sleep, characteristic of being in an active dream state. So, left for another day is the question: What does an unborn child dream about? And that's the way it is, March 6, 1975."

The knocking on my front door was neither loud nor in rapid staccato. Three quick raps from the unseen knuckles. I rose from my couch, its leather upholstery making a soft 'whoosh.' Side-stepping the coffee table, in four steps I was across the living room to the door. Cautious as all city dwellers, I peered out the small rectangular window mounted high up in the door. I could just see the top of a head covered in straight brown hair.

No threat here. I swung the door open, the big hinges creaking as it pivoted in its customary arc. Two teen-aged girls, one visibly pregnant, broke into smiles. The not-pregnant teen removed a half-smoked cigarette from her mouth.

"I'm Sarah, Sarah with an 'H'. My car," and she pointed to a dented, two-tone Chevelle, "died on us. This is Misty. She's about to pop." Sarah flicked her index finger and thumb together to tap her friend's huge belly as if she was testing a melon for ripeness. Misty was obviously ripe. "And she really needs to pee. Could she please use your bathroom?"

The cigarette returned to Sarah's lips as I considered. During my momentary failure to bow and bid them entry, the two spoke to each other in hushed tones.

"It's OK, Misty. I'll find you some bushes. It won't be the first time you've peed in the bushes. Our ride will be here soon. Come on, let's just go."

Silent Misty had set the hook and reeled me in by my long-cultivated sense of protection for pregnant women. As they began to turn away, Sarah blew smoke in my direction. "Sorry we bothered you."

I felt ashamed. "No, please come in. I'm sorry I didn't respond quicker." I smiled, stepping out of the doorway. "I'm Bruce. Please put out your cigarette before you come in. The bathroom is straight through the dining room, down the hall, first door on the left. Go. When you're done, you both can wait inside, if you want, until your ride arrives."

Misty bee-lined past me. Sarah, smelling of smoke, stepped inside. She looked around.

"Sit wherever you like,' I said, closing the door.

She slouched down into one of the wing-backed chairs that flanked the couch. I resumed my usual place on the right-hand corner of the brown leather sofa.

Out of my sight, Misty was busy in the bathroom. First, she searched the medicine cabinet for drugs, then the vanity drawers. Next the sink area, checking for rings, watches or other valuables that might have been temporarily removed. Her routine was practiced and perfect. Slowly and quietly she opened the bathroom door. My bedroom had to be on her left. With her back to the hallway wall, Misty moved toward her objective. She checked the nightstand first: maybe drugs or a gun. Next would be the dresser top and drawers. Score! My dress watch, an Omega, she palmed in her right hand. Smooth and fast. Finally, to sell the deal, a quick return to the bathroom and a flush of the unused toilet. They'd both be long gone before I even knew I'd been had.

* * * *

Sarah and I hadn't been speaking. She surveyed the room while I watched the local news. When I got up to change the channel, I noticed her partner sneaking down the hall. I immediately headed towards her.

"You've got a nice place here and you were sweet to help my friend." Sarah's words spilled forth as she rose from her seat, trying to distract me. Ignoring her, I moved across the living room toward Misty.

"Hi Misty, what's up? Run out of toilet paper, or just having a look around in my stuff? I think you both need to leave; let's go." I held my place in the hall as she turned and headed back to the living room. When she passed by me, I saw the watch clutched in her hand.

I grabbed her wrist and extracted my Omega from her palm. "You'll stand right here." I took two steps back through the dining room to my kitchen doorway. The beige wall phone was now in easy reach.

Sarah, the alpha of the pair, moved quickly into the dining room, her hands out, palms up. They'd been caught in the act before, so there were contingency plans already prepared.

"Misty what did you do?" Sarah asked in mock surprise. "We are so sorry. Can we please just go? You'll never see us again."

I reached for the phone.

"Please, Misty doesn't want to have her baby in jail." Sarah paused, waiting for my response. When none came, Sarah upped her plea. "And I'm pregnant too."

I ignored her and started to dial.

"Hey, wait. Have you ever had a pregnant chick? She'll do yah, doggie style. If that doesn't turn you on, you can have me instead, anyway you want." She lightly brushed her tongue onto her lips. Moving her hands from the 'wait' gesture, she began to slowly unbutton her blouse. "Or do you want to be greedy and have us both? Right, Misty?"

I turned to finish dialing.

With my back to her, Sarah moved on to their fail-safe plan of last resort. Reaching under the hem of her blouse, she pulled out an improvised sap: lead fishing weights inside a wool sock.

The first blow caught me over my right ear. Stunned, ear bleeding, I dropped the receiver and reached for the wall to stay upright. The sap returned with a backhand swing that bloodied my scalp. My vision went black. As I collapsed onto the floor, the final strike hit above my right eye. I neither felt the pressure that made my eye bulge nor heard the dull, wet crack as my skull gave way. You see, death is painless; it's getting there that's a bitch.

Sarah stepped into the kitchen, being careful not to put her shoe into the slowly widening pool of blood. Leaning down, her lips just above my face, she looked and listened for any sign of life. Seeing none, she whispered in my ear with the sweetness of a lover, "That'll learn yah."

Misty grabbed the watch from my dead hand while Sarah urged her toward the door. Their pink and primer-gray Chevelle ran just fine. They would be long gone, hopefully unseen by neighbors as they escaped.

* * * *

Misty, the pregnant thief, had her baby two weeks later in the county hospital. She'd call him 'Soc' for short; an inside joke shared with Sarah, the sap lady.

Sarah had lied to me when I was still alive and it suited her goals, but she had been truthful about her pregnancy. The same soul that had been Bruce in my last life entered her womb during the 20th week after conception. Possessing a soul, I was now more than a ball of cells or a pink peanut. My eye stalk had moved from the sides of what would be my head. My soon-to-be skull bones converged to make a crude but recognizable human face. And I began to dream. Dreaming kept me mostly still. I shared Sarah's drinks and her conversations as a quiet, ever-present listener.

Sarah and Misty were lovers. Much of what I heard through the thin layers of flesh that separated my soon-to-be new body from the outside world was pillow talk that came to invade my dreams of my last life. These dreams were a wordless movie of that life, seen through the eyes I'd once possessed: views from inside my head, looking out.

Language is a function of each incarnation and not built into our unborn brain, but not so with the unique sound of a voice.

"You're so good. God I want you, oh-oh don't stop."
The words of love and lust that flowed, sometimes
quietly, sometimes explosively between the two
women, over time registered in my dreams. The soft
sounds of love that penetrated Sarah's abdomen were
by the same voice as those in my last memory. "That'll
learn yah." Bruce's final sights and sounds fused into my
unborn dream.

* * * *

The first sounds of my latest incarnation were neither
sweet nor gentle. "Oh shit this hurts! Where's my
epidural? Get this kid out of me." As I passed from the
dark to the light, my new Mom grew quiet. Here I was
again, out of the one great sea of birth and death, dirty
and crying, as unseen hands lifted me to Sarah's breast.
This time, I'd be named William. Following Misty's
model for naming children, 'Bill' suited Sarah because
that was what I represented, as she intended, for her
baby's Daddy: a monthly bill to be paid.

Sarah had loved her baby's Daddy deeply: in fact to
the exact depth of his wallet. Sarah never had sex with a
woman for money or with a man for free. Conception
had been part of her plan; marriage had not. Baby Bill
represented a small cash cow for her. Baby Bill received
all the care that he required to secure the continuity of a
cash flow. Her little investment was not so much loved
as tolerated and protected.

* * * *

The same dream was always there, stuck in my head, for as long as I can remember. When I was very little, the dream was a single image; Bruce's body on the floor, blood pooled beneath it; and the voice, soft as a caress, 'That'll learn yah." It came to me unbidden and then went away. But it always came back, sometime days, sometime weeks later, whenever I heard the same voice. But the caressing voice was never addressed to me. That voice was saved for my other mom, Mommy Misty.

Soc, my older brother, was the product of an industrial accident, we decided years later when we became old enough to understand the crude humor of 'The Moms' that we overheard.

"Well, next time don't buy those cheap rubbers; I told you they'd break right during your second faked 'big O'," Sarah teased Misty as they sat on the balcony of our apartment drinking beer. "Baby, you should have bought the radial plies; they give you a lot better mileage." She belched and tossed her empty beer can into the remnants of a cardboard box already overflowing with dead Keystone Lights.

"Yeah, well I figured him for a short hitter; one look at my tattoos, half a dozen pumps, three moans, and he'd bust his nut."

With only one bathroom and the Moms' indifference to modesty, Soc and I had both seen Mommy Misty's twin tattoos, a 'W' on each cheek of her buttocks. When her customer took her from behind, she'd spread her cheeks to spell "WOW. If the date took her missionary style, she'd raise her legs into the air so her inked greeting became "MOM."

"Billy, get me another beer and turn that god damn TV down," Sarah called over her shoulder. I left Soc's side in front of our electronic baby sitter and ran to the kitchen. Holding my nose, I passed through the ammonia vapor cloud and sidestepped the dirty cat box. Mommy Sarah didn't take being ignored very well; not that being told to fetch beer was the only attention I got from her. She also said: "Turn the god-damn TV down; go play outside," and my favorite, "Go to bed, you little bastard!"

Soc and I liked watching TV best because we were mostly left alone. I also liked "Go to bed," even with the "you little bastard" added. Years before I knew what a bastard was, Mommy Sarah's tone told me it meant 'hide.'

Soc and I shared one small room: bunk beds, one dresser, and a perpetually overflowing hamper of dirty clothes. Our cat, Benny, would curl up near my head as I drifted off under my single quilt. Benny's warm body helped ease me into the escape of my dreams. If the Moms were in their bed and that certain sweet tone penetrated the thin bedroom walls, the dream—the man, the blood and the Mommy Sarah's cooing, "That'll learn yah"—all came back to me. As I got older, tutored by television and some silent recognition from deep inside myself, the dream morphed into a private puzzle that lingered into my wakefulness.

Soc and I both found refuge in front of the TV. We liked Sesame Street. The Muppets were kind and happy, two things that were in short supply at our house. Muppets wanted to teach us: to get along, learn our alphabet and colors, and to be safe. They sang about danger and Elmo showed us how to stay safe around cars and traffic. I loved watching, 'Safety Counts on Sesame Street.'

What stuck in my little mind the most, probably due to its repetition, was a show for parents, 'Safety Tips for Parents and Caregivers.' As I listened to this week's repeat of safety tips, the final piece of the dream, the voice and the words, all fit together into a complete picture. Mommy Sarah had murdered the person that I had been. Even in my six-year-old mind there was an understanding that I shouldn't share the dream with Mommy Sarah. So, not knowing what to do with my new-found epiphany, I put it aside for the safety of TV and kindness of Sesame Street.

Burt and Ernie taught us about safety around guns and how guns can kill people. But there it was, unescapable in my little mind. Guns kill people. Mommy Sarah kills people. If I told anyone, like my first grade teacher, Mommy might kill me too! When the dream and the full picture started coming to me more often, I began to wet my bed. The Moms stopped letting me drink anything after dinner, but it didn't help. Waking me up in the middle of the night didn't help either, nor did their frustration that lead to shaming and spankings. "You lazy little bastard, I know you can stop pissing the bed if you wanted."

* * * *

First grade was a refuge, just like TV. Soc and I sat side by side watching Sesame Street after school. Benny the cat slept in the hollow between my knees as I sat cross-legged on the floor. The 'Parents and Caregivers Tips' made their weekly appearance. And there it was. I'd listened to the tips many times before without really hearing one particular part.

"Water and electricity don't mix. If you're in the bathtub or shower, or standing on a wet floor, never touch anything electrical, like a light switch or hair dryer."

"Billy"—I ignored the summons, lost as I was in the video world. "Billy!" a scream this time. "Get in here; Mommy needs cigarettes." Roused from the TV, I tried to rise slowly without disturbing my best friend, the cat. As the third "Billy" sounded, I appeared in the bathroom door. Mommy Sarah was in the tub, sitting upright the better to smoke, her breasts just above the soapy water and one forearm resting on the four-inch wide porcelain edge of the tub. A red plastic ashtray balanced there, just inches away from her fingers.

"God damn it, are you deaf?" Softening her tone now, she pointed to the bathroom vanity, just out of reach, six inches away from the edge of the tub. "Hand me my cigarettes and bring me another beer."

I chose to fetch the beer first.

In the kitchen, my eyes watered from the ever-present ammonia fumes that hovered above Benny's cat box. I grabbed a single Keystone Light and closed the refrigerator door, all the while holding my breath. The sounds of happy singing filtered in from the living room and I wanted to be safely back on Sesame Street. But there would be no peace until the beer in my hand was delivered.

Back to the bathroom I went, handing the can, now slippery with condensation, to Mommy Sarah. "Now, the cigarettes," she ordered as the beer can opened with an audible 'pop' and a small splash of foam. A half-full pack of Salem Menthols sat where she'd pointed, next to her hair dryer, plugged in and sitting at the side of the sink. I picked up the cigarettes and handed them to her.

"Mommy, Sesame Street says that cigarettes are bad and can kill you."

"Yeah, whatever," was her response as she carefully set down the beer, trading it for a blue Bick lighter. "Get the hell out." Cigarette lit, she dropped her right hand back under the soapy surface, the better to enjoy her smoke, beer and a little ménage a mono.

As I turned, the bathroom door to my right, vanity on my left, the dream came fully into my mind's eye, and I stopped. "Get out," she repeated, her voice just below a yell. I looked at her and then at the vanity. The hair dryer beckoned as Mommy Sarah swatted out with her cigarette-filled hand. But in that instant I didn't feel the heat of the glowing tip. I only saw her crouching above the dead body that had once housed the soul now reincarnated as her Billy. I heard again her words, "That'll learn yah." I flipped on the hair dryer, it's 'whirr' changing to a popping sound as it slid from my hand into the bath water. Mommy said nothing as she dropped her lit cigarette onto the ragged bath mat and died.

Standing now in the bathroom door, I carefully leaned over the tub to whisper, "That'll learn yah." The happy sound of song from the TV beckoned me back to the front room. Soc hadn't move and neither had Benny. Easing myself down to the floor I sat cross-legged behind Benny.

* * * *

When Mommy Misty found Sarah, she got to speak to a policeman. Soc and I had to talk to the police lady. She gave us each a stuffed bear in a blue 'Officer Friendly' uniform. The lady police told us she was so sorry that one of our mommies was gone because of a bad accident, but Mommy Sarah was now with God and we'd be OK. Soc and I were glad when all the police left because we could go back to TV.

Mommy Misty had never been mean to either of us. Maybe an unplanned birth makes less bad Karma than a birth as part of a moneymaking scheme. I'm hoping that without the bullying of dead Mommy Sarah, she'll be happier and nicer to us. I guess Soc and I will have to wait and see. Here's hoping that it's like at the end of the bedtime stories Mommy Misty tells us sometimes, "and they all lived happily ever after."

The End

Author's Notes

The two female characters are based on a pair of crime partners I supervised when I was a county probation officer in California before becoming a fed. The discovery of unborn babies dreaming is true and was big news when I was in graduate school in the early 1970's. My understanding of Buddhism, as explained by Bruce, is my own and also from my college days.

Also by This Author

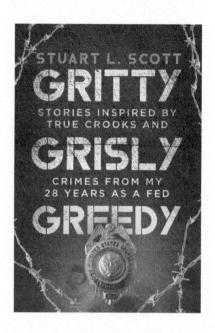

The Tooth Fairy
A story as cold as a Spokane winter about what happens
when a crook chooses the wrong victim.
The Grand Tetons
The Texas bank robber who carries twin 38's.
Idaho Catch and Release
Husband and wife pornographers who give a new
meaning to what's really a crime.
The Deal
The 1976 case of a crooked politician revisited in 2016.

Available at Amazon in paperback and on Kindle
ISBN:978-1-7322468-1-2

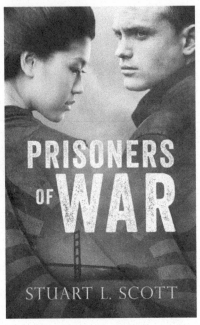

Prisoners of War is simultaneously a love story, a mystery and a history, all woven together. Everything of a historical nature is true to the best of my knowledge and research. Conflict between love and duty. Conflict between love of country and the love of your life. How far would you go to win back your love, when the government has taken her away? Fear, racism and abiding love collide in 1942 America, when your only crime was being born Japanese.

Available at Amazon in paperback and on Kindle

ISBN: 978-1-7322468-2-9

Why should you read this book? Do you want to start your own business, sell a product, or provide a valuable service? **Do you have a new business,** especially a small business? Do you like the idea of **learning from the insights or mistakes of others?** Or maybe you know me and want to see what stupid stuff I'm saying? Are you curious how I started with an $18,000 budget and a basement location in 1983, and ultimately sold the same business for $250,000 in 2011?

If you answered **YES** to any of these questions, then this book is for you—and it's a bargain. I learned long ago that I didn't have to be nearly as smart or creative when my mouth was shut. So I kept my mouth shut and my ears open, and I stole the good ideas of others. This is your chance to do the same!

Available at Amazon in paperback and on Kindle

ISBN: 978-1-7322468-4-3

Made in USA - Kendallville, IN
1183732_9781732246874
10.27.2020.0947